Murder Does
Light Housekeeping

MINNA BARDON

Murder Does
Light Housekeeping

MINNA BARDON

COACHWHIP PUBLICATIONS
GREENVILLE, OHIO

Murder Does Light Housekeeping, by Minna Bardon
© 2024 Coachwhip Publications edition
Introduction © Curtis Evans

First published 1941
Minna Bardon, 1900-1974
CoachwhipBooks.com

ISBN 1-61646-592-1
ISBN-13 978-1-61646-592-6

MURDER MOST MODEST

Murder Does Light Housekeeping (1941),
by Minna Bardon

Curtis Evans

Many tenants preferred to lodge without common meals or to live in larger, more anonymous rooming houses, where a "light housekeeping room" included a gas fixture for cooking on a single burner. In a rooming house residents could keep their own hours, enjoy greater privacy and perhaps entertain guests more easily. Landlords too could prefer lodgers to boarders for many of the same reasons. Boardinghouse families began to prefer their privacy to the affective ties of an extensive surrogate family.—"Boardinghouses," *Encyclopedia of Chicago* at http://www.encyclopedia.chicagohistory.org/pages/152.html.

"You can always tell a light housekeeping apartment by the pint of milk set on the window sill to cool. It is always a pint. Never a quart. . . . I think that the Italian boy who lives in a tenement is better off in every way—except, perhaps, in the matter of air space—than the light housekeeping American youth. He stands a much better chance of becoming president than does a young hopeful brought up in an apartment of two rooms who is taught that it is good form to scramble eggs in the bathroom."—Dr. Walter S. Goodale of Buffalo in testimony before the Twelfth New York State Conference of Charities

"We're all poor here, Mr. Burke—Riley and Dulcy and I, and all the rest of them. We make a little and we spend a little, and our rents have to be cheap. We have little house-keeping apartments made out of ordinary lodging house rooms. We cook our meals on little stoves. We go to market to buy our vegetables cheap. We make our own clothes."—Jane Robbins to Detective Inspector Burke in *Murder Does Light Housekeeping*.

The so-called Had I But Known (HIBK) suspense novel pioneered by bestselling American mystery writer Mary Roberts Rinehart (1872-1958) typically was set in large (if perhaps somewhat decayed) mansions occupied by genteel (if perhaps somewhat decayed) families of white Anglo-Saxon Protestant origin, possessors of impeccable family trees which likely boasted an ancestor who came over on the Mayflower in 1620, perhaps another who signed the West Jersey Concessions in 1676 and maybe yet another who in 1775 rebelliously peppered British lobsterbacks with buck and ball at the battles of Lexington and Concord. However, when Rinehart follower Minna Bardon (1900-1974) published the third of her four mystery novels, *Murder Does Light Housekeeping* in 1941, she took rather a different tack from her distinguished preceptress.

Bardon set her book in a house divided into what were then known as light housekeeping apartments, one-room abodes with a gas ring, sink and tiny, improvised pantry that allowed tenants to do their own modest cooking. This was a setting far more reflective of urban life as many Americans on the eve of World War Two actually lived it than those found in the novels of Rinehart or such prominent Rinehart disciples as Mignon Eberhart (1899-1996). If a great part of the appeal of the Eber-Rinehart mystery of the Depression years is witnessing the lifestyles of the rich and felonious, in Minna Bardon's books it is getting to glimpse how the proverbial "other half" endured their more economically precarious existences.

While Dashiell Hammett, as Raymond Chandler memorably declared, took fictional murder out of the Venetian vase and rudely dropped it into the alley, Minna Bardon hauled it from the drawing room into the light housekeeping apartment, in this case the domicile of unflappably good-natured eighteen-year-old secretary Jane Robbins, who maintains both her humor and her culinary aptitude throughout a series of murders that might well have made the toughest of Rinehart cookies clutch her pearls as she cowered on the fainting couch. (Admittedly, young Jane possesses nary a pearl to clutch, though she does claim a couch.)

"I was eighteen, then, young enough to take the unexpected in my stride," Jane recalls. "Sudden death, even murder, was horrible, frightening, but it was somehow exciting." Elsewhere she comments pugnaciously: "My brother taught me how to box, years ago, and I know just where to hit a man to do the most good, in the quickest amount of time." It should not surprise the reader that Minna Bardon, who was what singer KD Lang termed a big-boned gal, as a high school senior played center on her girls' center-ball team and was largely credited with achieving the beleaguered team's only victory that year.

In the tradition of HIBK mystery fiction, *Murder Does Light Housekeeping* is retrospectively narrated by Jane, who looks back, from some unspecified point in the present time, on the days when a series of murder struck the beleaguered tenants of her apartment building. "There were twenty of us in the house," she recalls. "It was a tenement, practically, made from an old mansion fallen on impecunious days, and we did light housekeeping, cooking on little stoves behind brave screens, with large talk about recipes and an undernourished air when we passed the big restaurants." Noting how when she was awakened by roomer Bill Broad ringing the doorbell in the early hours of one morning she got up to answer the door without turning on the light, she adds in foreboding HIBK fashion: "If I had put it on then, maybe I'd have seen the blood-stained coins early enough to get to the police before the second murder."

Not only is there a second murder, there is a third and a fourth and a fifth, not to mention two attempted ones (Jane tabulates all this mayhem late in the novel), making *Housekeeping* a surprisingly bloodthirsty tale even by modern standards, at least in terms of its murder rate. As Isaac Anderson wryly stated in the *New York Times Book Review*: "Enough corpses come to light in Mrs. Meyer's rooming house to furnish forth half a dozen mystery stories." Worse yet for Jane, it appears that the murderer is trying to set her up as the fall girl for the crimes—hence the bloody loose change deposited in her apartment, not to mention the bloodspots on her mantlepiece and bathrobe.

Largely the clues in *Housekeeping* turn on domestic details, especially those related to cookery. There are the exquisite lacy brown edges of Madame Terracci's crepe-thin pancakes, the paraffin seal atop the jam jar and the two loaves of experimental gingerbread, one with vanilla flavoring, the other with almond. Jane seems to spend a tremendous amount of time making coffee in her little pot for importunate young bachelors, and she is always running out of cream. Sometimes she pops open a can of sardines or makes some rolls to have something for them on the side. At one point she even manages a pot roast with carrots and potatoes. As a book reviewer in the *Detroit Free Press* put it: "Jane's ability as a cook got her out from under the finger of suspicion. She knew her pancake batter and pointed out that the murderer didn't know how to open a jelly [sic] glass, permitting authoress Minna Bardon to prove that when 'Murder Does Light Housekeeping' . . . it's bound to be tripped up."

****

"Authoress" Minna Bardon was born Minna Shubinski Feibleman in Cincinnati, Ohio, on July 18, 1900, to Harry and Lillian Feibleman (nee Shubinski), one of the couple's three daughters. Harry managed modestly to support his family as a commercial traveler in such gentleman's articles as cigars and sock garters, but his eldest girl Minna, the prodigy of the family, after her graduation from Hughes High School in 1918 paid her way through the University of Cincinnati by teaching English to immigrants at Cincinnati's Jewish Settlement House and working summers at the Fresh Air Farm, a recreational camp for underprivileged city children. During her senior year at Hughes High School, the outgoing and confident Minna had served as President of the German Club—possibly a bold act after American entry into the Great War in opposition to the Central Powers—and as center on the girls' center-ball team.

Her Hughes classmates nicknamed Minna—a big, tall girl who towered over her center-ball teammates—"Billie" and, doubtlessly ironically, "Tom Thumb." (This followed the principle of inevitably dubbing a huge male classmate "Tiny.") While at the University of Cincinnati Minna served as Secretary of the Menorah Society and the Cosmopolitan Club and a Director of the Young Women's Hebrew Association. After graduating from college in 1922, she worked in advertising, served as a staff member with *Writer's Digest* and book reviewer with the *Cincinnati Enquirer* and wrote fiction—romance, science and mystery—for the pulps. She published work under her own name, Minna Feibleman, and at least one pseudonym, Phyllis Lee. Two early mystery novelettes which she published under her own name were "Tear-Gas" and "Dining with Death," these appearing successively in March and April 1930 in *Dragnet* (later *Detective Dragnet* and *Ten Detective Aces*).

On July 27, 1931, three months after the passing of her widowed mother, with whom she had lived, Minna, then thirty-one years old, wed twenty-eight-year-old Emanuel Bardon, founder and owner of the Bardon Printing

Minna is easily spotted as the 'center' of her team.

Company. The marriage, which was solemnized by re-
form rabbi Victor E. Reichert of Rockdale Temple (later
a great friend of poet Robert Frost), was kept a simple
affair due to the death of Minna's mother and, quite possibly, the precarious state of the couple's finances. Up until
his somewhat late blooming romance with Minna (for the
time), Emanuel, the son of a Jewish furrier, had resided
in Cincinnati with his widowed mother, grandmother and
two brothers. Emanuel simply moved from his mother's
house into Minna's late mother's home on 232 East Ro-
chelle Street, not far from the University of Cincinnati.

Within four years of her wedding Minna had given birth
to the couple's twin girls Lillith and Janice and their son

Harry, yet still she persisted in writing fiction. This was not simply a matter of personal whim on her part, for less than a year into their marriage Emanuel commenced bankruptcy proceedings both for his business and personally for himself. Things soon looked up somewhat, however. The Bardon Printing Company managed to reconstitute itself and in 1937 Minna published her first full-fledged detective novel, *The Case of the Dead Grandmother* (reprinted in paperback as *Murder for Real*). This was soon followed, in 1939 and 1941, by *The Case of the Advertised Murder* and *Murder Does Light Housekeeping*. Minna clearly was doing her share—and then some—to support her family.

Nonetheless, a 1937 *Cincinnati Enquirer* profile highlighted how houseproud and devoted to thrifty domesticity Minna was. Rather like frugal Jane Robbins in her mystery novel *Murder Does Light Housekeeping*, Minna did "all her own cooking" and baked "the bread her family eats," in addition to making "most of her own and the children's clothes." The photo which accompanied the article showed an ample, much filled-out Minna sitting in a chair with her trio of kinder around her, a Peter Pan picture book in her lap, while Emanuel, coatless and balding in necktie and braces, retiringly looked on over his wife's shoulder.

Three years later, in another *Enquirer* profile, Minna frankly admitted that life in the Thirties for her and Emanuel was an ongoing economic struggle, though one which she, with her restless zest for life, relished. The interviewer made note of Minna's mystery writing and other work outside the home, yet again emphasis was placed on the author's skills as a home economist. Minna was quoted saying: "I have the two largest bread-mixing bowls in Cincinnati, and I make all my own bread. My husband raises our own vegetables and some fruit and I [preserve them] . . . probably I'm the only woman under

65 in the city who still carries a string bag." She added wryly: "People who have the idea that you're wealthy because there is a novel in the library bearing your name are mistaken. I manage to keep three steps ahead of the sheriff, take care of my home and husband and children, and thank goodness I have a sense of humor."

With America's entry into World War Two, Minna more than ever needed that positive outlook on life. Her mystery writing lapsed, though she kept up her book reviewing. Like so many other Americans at the time, she and her husband found themselves struggling with a succession of overseas family calamities. Emanuel's older brother Robert died in Normandy on the day after D-Day, while his younger brother Clifford, a radio operator and gunner on a flying fortress, soon afterward was shot down and captured in France, after months of captivity becoming the first Cincinnatian freed in a prisoner-exchange. Meanwhile Minna's nephew Bernard Harry Simpson, her sister Esther's only child, was killed in action at Serrig, Germany, near the border with France in March 1945, a bare ten days after his arrival in Europe. Bernard was only eighteen, a thin, gangling, bespectacled boy with a big grin, judging from his Hughes High School senior class photo, which was taken less than a year before his tragic demise across the ocean in an old world of ageless, irrational enmities.

Minna rallied to publish a final detective novel, *Blood-Red Death*, in 1947. After Emanuel passed away at the age of fifty-five on All Hallow's Eve in 1958, Minna, now a fifty-eight-year-old bird with an utterly empty nest, with all of her characteristic energy took up social work, becoming, just a few days before her sixtieth birthday, an employment consultant with the Hamilton County Welfare Department.

Her goal in taking on this employment, she told the *Cincinnati Enquirer* in 1966, was "to help people make

the most of their own ability." She still insisted, nonetheless, that "I've always got some mystery or suspense story
in mind," warmly recalling: "When I was real young my
mother used to read detective stories aloud to my father.
. . . The whole family listened." Her first story had been
a Halloween tale, ironically enough (given her husband's
later death on that holiday), written when she was twelve
and published in a children's magazine. With striking
practicality, born of the circumstances of her challenging
life, she added: "I didn't start writing for the fun of it. I
wrote for the cash in it." A fiction traditionalist, Minna
disdained the franker tenor of modern crime writing,
declaring: "It used to be they insisted on keeping sex out
[of genre fiction] because readers were mostly kids. Nowa-
days they write for those who are adult at least in years—I
won't say emotions."

MINNA BARDON

The 1966 *Enquirer* profile described Minna as "a jolly woman with infectious laughter—when she's around you realize her presence. . . . Her hair is silver now, but her eyes sparkle with excitement when she discusses her writing or her present work." She happily told her interviewer: "The only thing I wonder now is why I didn't get the [social work] job sooner. I think there are an awful lot of women who would like this sort of thing, especially after their children no longer need all their time. . . . there's always a chance you might do some good for somebody."

In the interview Minna called for establishing public day care centers in Cincinnati, allowing single mothers to take employment and get off city welfare rolls. "There are two ways to get people off the rolls," she pronounced. "One is to kick them off and the other is to get them jobs so they can earn independence." Minna, an old progressive from the days of Jane Addams' Hull House, advocated for the latter hopeful way.

Minna Bardon never published another novel, but when she died in 1974 at the age of seventy-three, she must have had the satisfaction of knowing that with her well-lived life she had done good for some people—working mothers and mystery readers alike.

This one is for Harry

1

There was such a slim chance of murder coming to the tall dark rooming-house that night. And yet murder struck again and again, not only at Miss Lizzie, who deserved to die horribly if anybody did—and I'm cold-blooded enough to recognize that—but at the rest of them who had hoped to live for so many more years.

There were twenty of us in the house. It was a tenement, practically, made from an old mansion fallen on impecunious days, and we did light housekeeping, cooking on little stoves behind brave screens, with large talk about recipes and an undernourished air when we passed the big restaurants.

The carved white marble mantelpiece in my room had probably been chosen in Italy a hundred years before the night the blood splashed on it, and the doors were of some heavy dark wood almost impervious to the screams of murder on that long-ago night.

Hours before the man stood on the doorstep in the storm, I heard the quarrel between Dulcy and the drug clerk, and I think I knew from that minute something was brewing in the house, even at that time, to cause the desperate note in Dulcy's voice, and the clipped menacing tone of the boy. I couldn't hear their words, only their voices, and they put over their meaning to me in the same

way you'd understand a quarrel between two people speaking
an alien tongue. Later I remembered the moan in Dulcy's
last words, and I thought I heard: "Milton! Milton!" which
was strange, because the drug clerk's name was Henry.

It was two-thirty in the morning when the shrill note
of the house doorbell cut through the silence. It wasn't the
first time that I'd had to get up and open the hall door to a
roomer who had lost his key. The landlady was deaf, and it
was easier to open the door myself than to try to call her.
Blankly I pushed myself out of bed, only half awake, and
padded toward the door in my bare feet because I didn't
want to put on the light and hunt my slippers. If I had put
it on then, maybe I'd have seen the blood-stained coins
early enough to get the police before the second murder.
But I walked through the dark, more unafraid than I've
ever been since, at night, and murder walked with me.

I could see that he wore dinner clothes and looked familiar, when I saw the man on the doorstep, but I couldn't
recognize him for a minute. I just stood there, probably
looking as stupid as I felt, with my hair straying over my
shoulders and my bathrobe inside out from being put on
in the dark. I didn't discover that until later, which is why
the little bloodstain on the pocket didn't make a clue for
me, but anyhow the man looked at me with more curiosity
than apology for waking me out of a night's sleep.

"You're Jane, aren't you, on the first floor in the big
room? I've been to your parties. I'm Bill Broad on the
third floor. You called me to the phone the other day. Remember?"

"Yes. I remember." I had answered the phone for everybody in the place, but that's what I got for living in a
place where there was a deaf landlady and a telephone
outside my door.

Conversation at two-thirty in the morning can be brilliant or a tragedy, according to what you've been doing

up until that time. I'm not at my best at the beginning of the day. Even nine o'clock is a nightmare until I've had my coffee, and it was far from coffee-time that night, although I didn't know it then.

Bill Broad went on talking without saying anything important. At least it wasn't important to me then, although I've wondered since whether I could have found the murderer earlier if I hadn't stood there half asleep on my feet, while Broad talked on and on about not having changed his keys when he changed his suits, and how enlightening a time he'd had roaming the streets talking to derelicts after the theatre. There are people who get fun out of finding out how the other half lives, but I've been too close to that other half too many times to go around asking questions of people with shabby clothes and hungry eyes.

I got back to bed and was asleep before a clock could tick twice.

When the knock came on the door and woke me, I thought that it sounded imperative, commanding me to hold audience with something outside the limited margins of my life.

I sat up in bed and clutched the covers around me. There was something uncanny about that knock in the dark. But the more fool I, I didn't turn on the light this time either.

"Who—is it?" My voice sounded strange to my own ears.

The room seemed suddenly very big and very empty and very cold. I reached for my bathrobe and put it on again, right side out this time, and by chance found the slippers that I hadn't been able to find the first time. Fortified by my clothes, I asked again: "Who is it?"

"It's me again—Broad. Something's wrong upstairs. I passed Miss Lizzie's door, and she's dead."

I'm ashamed to think that my first emotion was one of relief. Then Betty would be happy again, or as happy

as she could be without her baby. And there would be no
more of the war that is inevitable when a high-spirited
young woman and a bigoted old maid are cooped up in
the same light housekeeping room, and the young woman
considers that the older one is responsible for her baby's
death. Putting it down that way makes it sound incredible
but that was all I kept thinking. Now Betty would be free
and Torry would come back to her and they'd be happy.

I went over and stood close to the door. The old red
carpet was stiff under my soft slippers. I thought I could
hear the man's heavy breathing on the other side of the
door.

"But—I can't do anything. Get a doctor. Why did you
call me?"

"The doctor wouldn't do her any good. She's dead, not
sick."

I felt a queer sweet taste in my mouth and sharp prick-
les of fear in the finger-tips that clutched my robe around
my body. I was terribly afraid, although I didn't know
why, and very cold, too. I started shivering, and my teeth
were chattering.

"Get somebody—a doctor—or the police—or somebody. There's a telephone right outside my door."

"Yes," Broad said. "I know. But it's a nickel phone and
I haven't any money. That is, I have bills, but I haven't any
change. I gave all mine to the taxi driver. I can't put a bill
in the telephone. Got a nickel?"

"No," I found myself saying absurdly, suddenly much
amused and not at all frightened, "you can't put a bill in
a nickel phone, I haven't a nickel, but will a dime do?" I
had found a dime in my bathrobe pocket, and I opened the
door just far enough to poke out the hand that held the
coin, before I began to wonder what the dime was doing
in the pocket. Certainly I hadn't put it there, and nobody

else went around putting dimes in bathrobe pockets, not even multi-millionaires.

I noticed that Bill Broad's fingers, as they touched mine, were hot and wet. Maybe he was afraid too. I stood there for a minute, with the door open a crack, watching him in the dim light from the hall globe. He took the phone off the hook and put the dime in and I heard a little double bell. He said into the phone:

"Give me the nearest police station. I don't know the number. I want to report an accident."

He gave the address and his name and hung up the receiver, as somebody came down the stairs.

It was that newspaper reporter from up next to Miss Lizzie's room. As a newspaper reporter I didn't know much about him, although he had come to my parties too. He wasn't the kind who has bylines or syndicates columns to small town newspapers, but there was something almost fictional about his cockatoo crest of red hair, his shabby bathrobe with the hole in the elbow, and the flapping carpet slippers on his bare feet.

I was so much interested in watching him come down the stairs that it didn't occur to me until five minutes later that Broad hadn't called the police at all, but had only spoken to the operator.

But that five minutes was almost the most eventful period of the night. We were on our way up to Miss Lizzie's room where she knelt dead.

And now this red-headed boy took out of his mouth the pipe he probably chewed on even while he slept, and said with a sort of undertone of excitement:

"Broad, do you know about Henry?"

"Henry? What's he done? Eloped with Dulcy?" Broad seemed mildly interested, like a man who stops to look into a shopwindow at a suit that's nowhere near his size.

"No. He's dead!"

"But it isn't Henry," I explained patiently. "It's Miss Lizzie who's dead."

"Yes. But it's Henry, too. He's dead. I didn't know about Miss Lizzie. Is it her heart?"

"We don't know. Broad came down and phoned the police. They're on their way here," I said hopefully, not quite knowing how they would get there if Broad had not reached them. I felt rather wobbly, as if I had had too many cocktails, and facts weren't quite straight in my mind.

Broad said in a voice of peculiar colorlessness, as if the words were being born out of a dictionary instead of a throat: "Miss Lizzie is dead on her knees, in an attitude of prayer. She is crying. And she glows in the darkness, like a ghost of a Neon light. I'll call the police again and hurry them. You go up and take charge, Riley. A reporter ought to know the ropes. Miss Lizzie and Henry, both at once. Maybe there's a connection. Take charge till the police get here. Give me a nickel for the phone, Riley?"

You could just see Riley hesitating between the two important jobs. Should he go up and take charge of the two dead bodies and try to find out whether the deaths were a suicide pact or two accidents or perhaps a suicide and a murder, or should he go down and call the police and maybe get himself patted on the back by a policeman who knew him vaguely as a reporter who filled in when the regular police reporter was on vacation?

The two corpses won.

He reached into the pocket of the slacks he wore under his shabby bathrobe and handed Broad a sparse handful of change. Broad went down the stairs three steps at a time and I could hear him take the receiver off the hook and start shouting things into the mouthpiece. This time he seemed to have the police station, so I stopped worrying about him and followed Riley upstairs.

And then we saw Miss Lizzie.

Her room was dark, and as we stared into it from the lighted hall, we could see nothing except a dusky glow surrounding something that looked like a low chair beside the bed.

It wasn't quite a light, not a spotlight, anyhow, but just a certain blue luminous quality to the darkness.

Then Riley pressed the light and we saw Miss Lizzie.

She was facing the door, kneeling beside the bed, and from the handkerchief that was pressed to her mouth, I thought that she had died while she was saying her prayers and crying at the same time.

God knows that she had enough to cry about and that she needed praying for, because a more despicable old woman it has never been my bad fortune to meet. Even in death there was about her the aura of something disagreeable, rather than the awe of death.

Then, in spite of all the horror of the night, I almost laughed at myself.

Because the aura that surrounded Miss Lizzie was a thoroughly nauseating blend of two unromantic scents, chloroform and garlic. Yes, garlic, as strong as the breath of the bricklayer who was fixing the wall at the corner.

I had never seen anybody dead except my old aunt and my great-grandfather, who had been old and majestic in death as he had been in life, with perhaps a little added serenity and majesty.

But Miss Lizzie was different. I could see very little of her face, because of the hand that held her handkerchief to her mouth. But the mean lines around the mouth and the shrewd malicious expression around the eyes were still there in spite of death. She was crouched in prayer, but there was nothing religious about her attitude, just as there had been nothing really religious about the bigoted sect that she had commanded.

She looked like a bird of prey crouched over a kill, and I kept thinking of Betty's baby who had fallen a victim to Miss Lizzie's theories as readily as if she had really been the rapacious harpy she seemed.

As I thought of Betty she came into the room, small and silent and fragile, her head held high as if her pride could keep her from giving way to emotion.

I put out my arms to her and she came into them. I felt motherly, the way you do when you're eighteen and you see another girl in trouble and want to help her, and I led Betty over to the chintz-covered divan in the corner and piled pillows up behind her and held her hand until she began to look a little less frozen.

"Jane," Betty said, "I'm not sorry, not a bit. I hated her. She was a mean, hateful woman. She killed my baby and I hated her. You know I did. I'm happy that she is dead."

A voice came from behind us, Riley's voice: "Better pipe down, Betty. The police will be here soon. When they ask you questions, answer them, but don't come out with a speech like that or they'll have you behind the bars in five minutes."

"They can't put me in jail for hating her."

"They could put you in jail for killing her," Riley said gently.

"But I didn't. Tell him I didn't, Jane. I've thought about it often. Just before Torry left I would wake up in the night thinking how wonderful it would be if she would die. But she didn't—not them, while I still had my baby, before she killed my baby."

"God, what a story," Riley said wistfully, and I wondered whether he'd really write it, whether I'd spread poor Betty's emotions out on a newspaper page for women to gossip about over back fences and in the butcher shops while they were waiting for a choice cut off the loin or two pounds of hamburger.

"If you didn't kill her, Betty, who did?"

"Didn't she just die? She had a bad heart. She was always talking about it every time she wanted us to stop doing something we wanted to do."

But Riley said gently, shaking his head as he stood beside Miss Lizzie: "No, Betty. Miss Lizzie was murdered. I'd swear to that. Wait till the police get here. They'll tell you the same. I want to look at Henry now. Look here, girls, come out into the hall so I can lock the door. You oughtn't to be in here. The police want rooms of murder locked up."

He looked young and important and as untidy as a small boy playing in the mud, but he was so earnest that I obediently got up and started to pull up Betty by the hand. However, she sat as firmly as a two-hundred-and-fifty-pound politician.

"Listen, Jane," she said. "This is my home, this room, such as it is. I've lived here ever since Torry lost his job the month after we lost the baby. I've lived here with Aunt Lizzie when I had to love something, even if it was only the yellow paint on the furniture and the tearoses on the chintz, because I hated Aunt Lizzie so much that I had to find some balance in life. Anyhow, Aunt Lizzie or no Aunt Lizzie, I'm staying here, Bob Riley, and wild elephants couldn't pull me out of this room."

"Wild elephants couldn't," said Bob Riley placidly, still staring down at Aunt Lizzie, "but wild cops might. Well, goodbye, all. If the police get here before I get back, tell them that I gave my all but I couldn't budge you out of the death room." He banged the door after him with all the fury of a storm at sea, and at that minute I heard the beat of rain against the window panes and realized that it had been raining for some time. At the time that Broad had stood on the doorstep ringing the bell the storm had begun. Maybe the thunder and lightning had started earlier,

but not the rain. The lightning was flashing, the thunder
was roaring enough to shake the house, and if those cops
were on their way to the scene of the death, they were
certainly getting wet. I wondered whether policemen ever
carry umbrellas.

We sat there quietly for a few minutes. Outside the
door, footsteps were milling around, and I could hear
voices, and people going up and down the long stairway.

But the doors were heavy and I didn't hear much. Betty
stirred restlessly, and then sat up straight and looked out
of the window at the storm.

"Torrence was here tonight," she said in a heavy monotone. "He quarreled with Aunt Lizzie. That's why I left
and went out. I was afraid that if I said anything more or
listened to—to that woman—I'd—I'd kill her."

Betty looked down strangely at her hands, as if they
weren't a part of her at all. I didn't say anything because
there didn't seem to be anything to say. You can't comfort
a girl because her aunt is dead when she hated the aunt.

"But if you hated her, Betty, then why are you this way?
Why do you act so shocked, so worried, so—so terrible?
Anybody'd think that you knew who killed Miss Lizzie."

"I do, Jane. That's the hell of it. Torrence killed her.
I knew he was going to kill her when I walked out of this
room tonight and saw them sitting here hating each other
so much that the room was blue with it. Torry killed her.
Jane, what am I going to do? They can't make me tell
them, can they?"

2

Riley thrust his red hair past the door frame and said: "Come along out, Jane, with or without Betty. I need you?' He was still sounding important, but I went anyhow, because by this time I didn't seem to have much will of my own. Betty's room was peaceful, in spite of the figure of Miss Lizzie. The yellow paint with which she had disguised all the shabby old furniture was as bright as a June sun, and the roses made you almost forget the chilly night of storm. I didn't have a watch, and I had no idea whether it was two-thirty or three or four. Things had happened so quickly that I was still numbed.

Everybody was standing around, half dressed, like at a fire or an earthquake. Twenty people. No, not twenty, because Miss Lizzie and Henry were dead, and Betty was in her room. That makes three not there, and there were two of us, Riley and I, facing the others. And where was George?

Broad was still in his dinner clothes, and I noticed for the first time that his sleeves were a little damp, as if the rain had begun before he came to the door. Dulcy was all curls and tears and frilly lace negligee, a candy-box doll except for something a little predatory about the calculating look she turned on the men.

Mrs. Meyer the landlady was there, a middle-aged, deaf woman, with that Helen of Troy beauty and attraction that is ageless. How she ever came to her position as landlady of a sort of rooming house fitted up for light housekeeping is something that I had never heard. She was the only landlady I ever knew who didn't hold you like an ancient mariner with tales of former glory. But her beauty wasn't dimmed by age or deafness, nor by the horrors of the sleepless night, and she was dressed as carefully as a debutante in the first fifteen minutes of a dance.

The others were herded into corners and stood whispering curiously while Broad solemnly put a key in the lock of a door and ushered Riley and me into a room. I had never been in the place before. It was big, one of those studios made of three smaller rooms thrown together. There were three studio couches and odd pieces of old furniture grouped together to make a pleasant although not particularly individual apartment.

"It's my place, and Henry's and George's," Broad told me. "We have roomed together for the last month. Look, Riley, this didn't have anything to do with Miss Lizzie. That might have been almost anything, but this is just an open and shut case of plain suicide."

"Got a note?" Riley said sharply.

"I haven't looked. I didn't have a chance. You see, Riley, I passed Miss Lizzie's room when I came in tonight, and what I saw drove everything else out of my head. How'd you happen to know about Henry?"

"Well, Broad," Riley said thoughtfully, "I ran out of pipe tobacco and I needed a smoke and thought I'd borrow some from George. The door was opened a little, and I called, and then came in and turned on the light, and here he was."

"And where is George, Riley?"

"All right, Broad. I'll bite. Where is George? He hasn't been to bed. That's one thing. His couch isn't opened up at all, any more than yours is. Henry's is the only one of the three that's been slept in."

"And it's three o'clock in the morning, more or less. Listen, guys and gals, doesn't anybody around here ever go to bed, and say, did that lightning hit somewhere around here? That was the worst flash in the lot."

I was never afraid of lightning, myself, even if I was standing in the room with a dead man, but somehow the thunder got me that night. It seemed to growl and to threaten, as if it knew something we didn't know and was holding out on us.

"There's a note somewhere, Riley. I'll find it, if you give me a chance. This is suicide. It couldn't be anything else. And I know why he did it. It was a girl in the house. That much I know. Maybe it was Dulcy. And if it wasn't Dulcy, then it was Jane here."

Jane is me, of course, and I straightened up to all of my sixty inches and gasped out: "Why, Bill Broad, you know as well as I do that it couldn't ever have been me that any man committed suicide about."

"Well, I'm sure I don't know why. And come to think of it, Henry did tell me yesterday that you were the kind of a girl who'd be as pretty when you were forty as you are now at eighteen."

Broad's bold black eyes challenged my stare. He was lying, I knew, but I had no way of proving it. There had never been a word between Henry and me that was any more personal than a talk about the clouds that looked like rain or the crowd in the subway at Fourteenth Street.

Riley was thoughtful. "It's George I'm worried about," he said. "Looks bad for him, all this does. Look, did he know Miss Lizzie well? Could it have been possible for

George to murder both of them and then take it on the lam?" I'm not any too sure what "take it on the lam" means, but it sounded like flight to me, and guilty flight at that. But what did George have to do with Miss Lizzie? And besides it was Torrence, Betty's husband, who had killed Miss Lizzie. And Torrence didn't even know Henry.

"George is probably out at a poker party, Bob Riley, just as he is four nights out of five," I reminded him. "And Bill Broad was right, the first time. Henry probably killed himself because of a girl—Dulcy, maybe. She'd be that kind, I think." I had all the scorn of a Dutch-treat type of girl for the girl who takes everything from a man and gives nothing, not even herself. But men liked Dulcy, and maybe a weakling like Henry would kill himself over a little fool like that.

The room looked tidy, too tidy for death. Because surely murder didn't come tiptoeing into the room and tiptoe out again without leaving a little flurry in its wake. Henry lay there quietly on his bed, more rested than I had ever seen him in all the nervous love-ridden days I had noticed him with Dulcy. His eyes were open, and his lips were parted a little as if he were about to say good night before he closed his eyes.

But Henry was dead.

It didn't look like murder, or even suicide. It didn't look like death, but of course it was. Even I could see that. There was no blood at all, no stabbing or shot or poison vial or anything to account for Henry's step out of life into death.

There was a book lying on a table and a box of chocolates with the candy neatly arranged in rows. There was a picture of Dulcy with a pretty pout on her painted lips and a self-conscious cluster of curls on her head. And that was all.

It was all so much more peaceful than anything else I had seen that night and anything else that I would see in the next hour that I probably attach too much importance to the peace and the awe, the serenity in the room.

I was eighteen, then, young enough to take the unexpected in my stride. Sudden death, even murder, was horrible, frightening, but it was somehow exciting. It was the sort of thing that happened when you were living away from home in a big city where people had big passions and did big sinning. I was on the stage under the spotlight that was shining on Miss Lizzie and Henry, and on this Bob Riley who was so young and so important and so very knowing. He knew what to do, or I thought he did. I obeyed without objection every order he gave me without stopping to wonder why he gave it and what business he had investigating murders when the police were on the way and would probably haul both of us off to jail for poking our noses into things that were none of our business.

It was when I was feeling a little fey with the excitement that I looked down and saw the little pear-shaped spot of blood on the pocket of the bathrobe I was wearing. It had dried stiff and brown and was crisping a little around the edges. It couldn't have been anything but blood. Even iodine looks different.

And I couldn't imagine where it had come from. There had been two deaths, but not a drop of blood in either of them. Besides, it wasn't enough blood for anything serious like murder. A small nosebleed, for instance, or a stubbed toe or marked shin might produce almost that much blood.

It was on me, on Jane Robbins, and so far nobody seemed to have noticed it and so nobody was asking questions. Carefully I shifted my hand and transferred my handkerchief from one pocket to the other, arranging it carefully so that a corner covered the spot. Riley was talking to

Broad, and neither of them seemed to be paying any attention to me.

I was making a little list, in my mind, of unexplained things. The police and Bob Riley could take care of the big thing, the murder and Henry's death, whatever that was. But I had my own small list of mysteries. First the unexplained dime in my bathrobe pocket. Second the bloodstain. Third: why had Broad hung up the receiver without calling the police the first time and then called them back and given all details later? Fourth: why had Broad said that Henry was in love with "somebody" who might be me when I knew very well, and so did he, that the light of Henry's life was Dulcy?

The thunder crashed outside and the lightning seemed to light up the night outside the windows of the room. The electricity flickered and I thought for a minute that it was going to fail us, but it went on again, full strength.

"Struck somewhere near here, I guess," Broad said. "I got home just in time."

"So did the murderer," answered Riley. "If he's still hiding in this house we'll get him pretty quick, unless he isn't afraid of getting his tootsies wet."

And it was just at that moment that the lights chose to go out entirely. There was one vast roar of thunder, a vivid flash of lightning, and as darkness came on us there in the room of death, the thunder roared again.

I tried to remember, foolishly, whether the lightning or the thunder came first, as if it made any difference. But there we were, without light except for the lightning storm, and with screams coming from the hall outside the door.

Dulcy, of course. She could scream with as much fervor as a radio ghost, and she did it again and again, while I stood, trembling with excitement or maybe fear, in the darkness, with Henry's dead body within a foot of me and with Riley and Broad, both very much alive, grabbing at my arms as if to lead me from the room.

The hall was as dark as the room, when we got out to where the rest were. I couldn't identify anybody at all by voices, and I've never been able to feel my way through the darkness and know where I was going, the way some people can. So I held onto Bill Broad on one side and Bob Riley on the other, knowing that if I started to stumble down the stairs one of them would grab me.

Dulcy was still screaming, and when Dulcy screams, she screams. If you have ever heard talk about bloodcurdling yells and want to make a recording of one of them for any frightening purpose, all that you'll have to do is to get hold of Dulcy.

Dulcy stopped screaming and began to talk, instead, in that pathetic stagey moan that was as much a part of her as her blond curls. If I wanted to be a cat I'd say that it was just as natural as the curls, but I wasn't catty at eighteen, even if I am now.

"My Henry! He killed himself because of me," wailed Dulcy. "I loved him."

"She isn't keeping that a secret," said Riley, under his breath. "And not a tabloid reporter in the place—or a cop."

I felt Broad shift uneasily. "Those cops ought to be here," he said. "But maybe the storm held 'em up."

"I never heard of cops staying away from a scene of murder because they were afraid of the lightning," Riley said. "Maybe I'd better go down and call 'em again, or run down to the precinct station. I could get down there quicker than I could get a call through now."

"I'll go," Broad said, "and bring 'em back with me. You're needed here, Riley. I don't know how to handle this gang, and you do. My flashlight is in the drawer. I'll get it." He dashed back into the room where Henry lay and came back in a minute and handed the light to Riley.

"Wait, Broad," Riley ordered crisply, and Broad waited. "The police will get here in God's good time. We need you more here. Look, Broad, there may be a murderer loose in the house, and we need every able-bodied man we can get. Go down and get the station again and see if you can hurry 'em up, and then let's herd this gang up to my joint and keep 'em safe while we look. Two murders here tonight, Bill Broad, and there may be a third if we don't find the guy that did it."

It was good melodrama, on any stage. But then it sounded like words of wisdom delivered from the depths of sagacity. Riley was a newspaper reporter. Riley knew what to do. Riley had seen murders before. He had watched the police work. So we all followed Riley through the darkness, afraid of everything, sure of nothing except of this youngster who knew the ropes.

We found seats in Riley's big room, after he had lit the candles that he kept as ornament on the mantelpiece.

In the flickering light we all looked ghastly, and when the lightning outside the room flashed in a sort of purple-white spotlight effect on the assembly we looked like a circle of corpses sitting around uneasily awaiting Judgment Day.

Mrs. Meyer sat in a high carved chair, with her head leaning against the back and her hands firm on the arms. She had a quality of magnificent quiet, as if her beauty were held in leash by the darkness, but she might any minute burst into song, like an opera singer in the spotlight on the stage waiting for her cue. Not that I remember any opera where the soprano sits and waits for a chance to pour out her heart in song, but she looked that way, and not like the landlady of a fifth-rate rooming house that had been turned into light housekeeping apartments.

Then there was Dulcy, all curls and melting tears and little limpid moans. She had three of the boys from the

top floor grouped about her being protective and com-
forting, and somehow she was usurping the corpses' star
parts. Nobody was thinking or talking about Miss Lizzie,
and few of them mentioned Henry except as somebody in
love with Dulcy.

Those three boys were unimportant. I don't remember
their names, and they never did do anything more than
act as a sort of supporting cast for Dulcy. But there were
others there, in the big room, huddled on the bed, crumpled into chairs, whispering a little, even giggling in an
hysterical sort of way, now and then, like the audience to
a mystery play that's being acted out on a dark stage.

Twenty there had been to start with. The three boys
and Dulcy and Mrs. Meyer made five. Miss Lizzie and Betty made seven. Broad and Riley and Henry increased the
number to ten. George— No, George wasn't there at all.
Neither was Torry, Betty's husband, Miss Lizzie's nephew.
Twelve. The two honeymooners on the second floor were
away for a week-end. Fourteen.

That left six, and in the gathering shadows I tried hard
to make out who the others were. There was the Basque
lad with the limp and the haunted eyes with long dark
lashes. There was the tall blond German with the military
air and the scar across his cheek. There was the quiet little
ash-blond girl who roomed with Dulcy and whose name
was Kay Johnson. That left three. The mail carrier who
had studied for the ministry but who had got sidetracked,
somehow. And the middle-aged woman who had once been
a music teacher but who worked in a candy factory now,
Madame Terracci her name was. And the little grey man in
the hall bedroom—Smith.

That was all.

We were all there together.

Except Miss Lizzie and Betty, George and Henry and
Torry.

Then above our heads, like the sound of machine-guns spattering, came a strange sound. It might have been rats knocking down something in the attic. It might have been the rain on the roof, or winds hurling themselves at the chimneys. But it was noise in the darkness, and Mrs. Meyer sat up straight in her chair like a sleepwalker rising. And in a voice that was sepulchral, she said: "Henry!" and pointed straight at the door.

We turned to look where she pointed. She gave a little moan, and when we turned to her again, we saw her slipping down quietly from her chair.

Mrs. Meyer had fainted.

And then Dulcy again let out one of those screams that was one step worse than a midnight train howling in your ear.

"Henry!"

But Henry lad dead on his bed, sleeping his last long rest.

And we were there, in the darkness.

The thunder roared outside, and the lightning flashed, and we thought that the two candles almost made the room darker than no light at all.

Until suddenly, a great puff of air blew somewhere, as if somebody had opened a door.

The two candles flickered and went out.

We were completely in the dark.

3

It was at that minute I began to be afraid for myself. It wasn't just the general panic that would come to anybody, especially an impressionable girl of eighteen. There was murder in the house, and somebody had committed the murder and that somebody might be right there in the room with us. No. It was more than that. Maybe it was selfish and cold-blooded, but the murder of Miss Lizzie or even Henry didn't mean so much to me, because my own affections weren't involved. Miss Lizzie's death would have been a relief if she had only died safely in her own bed. And Henry, the drug clerk who loved Dulcy, was one of those wistful but vague young men fated to be unhappy in love.

Half of the love-suicides in history must have been like that. If Keats hadn't died of T.B., and hadn't written poetry, he might have been a little like that too, and maybe his Fanny was a little like Dulcy. I've always thought so.

But Henry wasn't a genius, and it was so logical for him to be a suicide that I didn't really believe that he had been murdered. After all, there was no evidence that I could see—nothing tangible, at any rate.

Now, however, I began to be afraid for my own life. The terror that seized me was probably due to the darkness and the storm as much as to the memory of Miss Lizzie, with that ghastly luminous aura around her.

But I was so mixed up in the whole thing. I had opened the door to the man who discovered one murder and roomed with the man who had died. I had a bloodstain on my robe. I had been chosen to go into the room with Miss Lizzie, and into Henry's room.

Why not one of the others? One of the men? Or Mrs. Meyers, who was older? Or Madame Terracci, the music teacher who now worked in the candy factory?

Now I wanted to pull myself away and I didn't know how. It was then that I began to suspect everybody. Not just Broad, who to me seemed most suspicious of all, but everybody. Mrs. Meyer. Even Riley. Where were the police? Had they ever been called at all? Were they on their way? Were all of the rooms up and downstairs empty, or in one of them was a man crouching? A murderer, waiting for somebody else to murder!

Maybe Torry hadn't killed Miss Lizzie. Maybe Henry hadn't killed himself. Maybe there was no connection between the two deaths except that the same man had committed both of the murders. Maybe he had a long list of candidates for murder.

Absurdly I felt a tune from *The Mikado* going through my mind, the one about the little list of people who never would be missed.

Miss Lizzie wouldn't be, or Henry. And a homicidal maniac who grabbed them for his first victims would have done less damage to the world than by the murder of almost anybody else in the house.

But who would come next? Fearfully I looked around the room. I couldn't see at all, except when the lightning flashed. Somebody had a flashlight, but it was pointed at the door at the stairway instead of at the people in the room. And then that went out.

If a giant finger had materialized out of the darkness, pointing at me and declaiming: "You'll be the next," I mightn't have been much more panicky than I was at that minute. I wondered if all the rest of them were feeling the same way.

Strangely we didn't talk, any of us—not even Dulcy, after that first scream, or Mrs. Meyer, who seemed to have come out of her faint as quickly as she had gone into it. Which was just as well, since none of us seemed capable of dealing with her, because we were all so scared ourselves.

Obviously both Dulcy and Mrs. Meyer considered that they had seen somebody who looked like Henry. Not his ghost, obviously, because surely not even Dulcy, who was pretty silly, could really believe in ghosts. Henry, appearing in the doorway, when we thought that he was dead. But he was dead, surely. Both Broad and Riley had said so. He had looked dead. Or had he? Had I just taken the word of two men who knew more than I did about death? Maybe he had been asleep and had since awakened. Maybe he had taken some sort of sleeping medicine so he had slept through the first part of the excitement and only awoke later when the thunder was especially loud.

Then everything was simple. Because we'd had only one murder, and we knew, Betty and I, that Miss Lizzie had been murdered by Torry.

There I was, torn between the panic of fright and the panic of bewilderment, not trusting anybody, all alone in the dark.

It was then that I decided, definitely, to creep out and sneak down to telephone the police myself.

I hadn't any idea how many of the others were still in the room. For all I knew, half of them might have been gone since the first five minutes we had come into the room. But I slipped out of my chair and felt my way to the door. The hall was long and narrow and the stairway had a firm banister. I held on tight to that banister and counted the steps all the way down, feeling my way as carefully as a novice skater on the ice for the first time. No reckless dashing downstairs in the dark for me. Nobody ever took longer to go down a flight of stairs. Twice I felt people brush past me, but whether they were going up or down, whether they were men or women, I hadn't any idea. I wasn't even quite sure that they were real and not figments of an overactive imagination.

My long bathrobe was a nuisance and I decided to change to a dress when I got downstairs. But first came the telephone to the police.

Finally I got all the way down and felt my way to the telephone. In the dark I fumbled for the receiver and took it off the hook.

The line was dead. I forgot that it was a nickel phone. For the first time I understood Broad's helplessness when he had knocked at my door and demanded the nickel for the phone.

I felt my way to my own room, and opened the door. I tried to remember where I had put the flashlight that I bought to send to Butch, my young brother, for Christmas. It was in the top drawer of the desk. I stumbled across the room, opened the drawer and grabbed out the package. No crimson tissue paper and silver ribbon was ever pulled from a package more quickly than I pulled that rustling stuff from the box that held the light. And when I finally found the catch and saw the little pencil of light wandering through the darkness, I came nearer to crying than I had since I was ten and somebody broke my doll.

The flashlight gave me confidence. I darted it around the room, happy to be in familiar surroundings once again. I saw my purse and the dress that I had had on and a few underclothes, and with no more light I managed to scramble into my clothes and tuck the purse under my arm.

I pushed the bathrobe back under some other things in the cupboard, debating whether I should cut out the bloodstain and flush that little piece of cloth down the toilet or whether I'd better leave it as it was and trust to luck that nobody would decide to examine the clothes.

I was clothed and in my right mind again, and I went out to the phone, armed with nickels this time, to call the police.

The line was dead.

I couldn't get the operator at all, although I used three nickels. Finally I made up my mind that the lightning had done something to it at the time the lights went out. I hadn't found my watch and I hadn't heard a clock strike, but it must have been four o'clock in the morning by this time. Maybe the rain would stop soon and the dawn would come and then this nightmare of death would end and we'd know what had really happened.

If I crept out of that hall door and into the storm I'd be mud and water in five minutes, even if I had umbrella, galoshes and raincoat. I could go back into my room and lock the door so that nobody could reach me. But how did I know that I would be safe, even there? Perhaps in some corner of my room lurked the murderer. I opened the door and slipped out into the hall again, knowing that I didn't want to go out into the storm, that I had no way of calling the police and that in all the house I didn't know one soul that I could trust.

No, that wasn't true. Betty could be trusted—my friend Betty, who had married Torrence and had a baby and lost it, and who always said that Miss Lizzie was the cause of her baby's death.

I made up my mind to go up to Betty's room, even if it meant sitting there with Miss Lizzie's body.

And then I heard footsteps coming down the stairs again. My flashlight went out and I waited. A small beam of light moved down the stairs, and feet moved along with it.

I saw the feet stop near the telephone wire about a
foot from the phone. Whoever it was put the light down
on a little table and bent to manipulate the wire, and as
he did this I could see that it was Riley—Bob Riley, with
his cockatoo crest of red hair and his know-it-all manner;
our young god of a reporter, who was running everything,
even murder. He had something shiny in his hand, maybe
a knife or a pair of scissors, and he was doing something
to the telephone wire.

Undoubtedly, I thought, he was cutting it. Now I
couldn't call the police at all, not even after the storm. Up
until then I hadn't seriously considered that Riley could
have had much to do with the murders, not really.

But if he was cutting the telephone wires so that nobody could reach the police, then surely he had plenty to
do with the dangers of the night.

I must have moved, or maybe my flashlight swung
against the door frame as I put it behind me, because he
suddenly rose and turned the light full force on me.

"Heh! So you decided to dress and become respectable,"
he hailed me. He tucked the shiny thing in his pocket before I could see whether it was knife or scissors, and I kept
my flashlight behind my back.

He went on talking in the same offhand manner, asking me how long I'd been downstairs and whether I'd seen
anything special. Of course I said that I'd only been down
long enough to dress in the dark, which takes twice as long
as dressing with a light on, and both of us laughed a little.
I hope that his laugh sounded more natural to him that
mine did to me.

I managed to get my flashlight into my big purse when
he turned his light toward the stairs to see if anybody else
was coming down.

Then he moved a little closer to me and spoke almost
under his breath. "Jane," he asked, "have you phoned the
police? Did they say that they had already sent somebody?"

"Oh no. I didn't phone anybody," I said, and it wasn't exactly a lie, because although I had tried to get the operator, I hadn't succeeded. And now maybe the police would never get there at all.

Maybe, I thought, with hysterical absurdity, we'd just stay there forever, with the storm thundering on outside and the corpses upstairs, and the lights out. Maybe this was our Purgatory. Maybe we were all dead and this was our punishment for our sins in our lifetimes.

But I pinched my arm hard and brought myself back to reality.

"I'll telephone," Riley said. Casually he went to the phone and took down the receiver. He tucked a nickel into the right space and I listened hard for the tinkle, but I couldn't hear anything, perhaps because just at that minute the thunder came louder than ever and Dulcy began to scream again, upstairs, as if murder had again come to our house.

Whether the tinkle came or whether it didn't, Riley went on talking into the telephone. After cutting the wire of a phone that was already dead (only obviously he hadn't known about that), he went on talking into the phone just as if it were working as usual.

"Police station," he said, after he dialed a number, "give me Burke of the homicide squad." He waited a minute and then went on: "Hi, Burke. This end—Bob Riley, of the *Standard*. You know, I took Kendall's place last month. Listen, did you get the report of the two murders at our place?"

I couldn't hear whether he had an answer, but he waited for a few minutes and then gave the address and a few particulars and said "Goodbye" before he hung up the phone.

More than anything I wanted to grab it and see whether it worked or whether this had been a phony call, but I couldn't find an excuse. As if he could read my mind, Riley said briskly: "Better not use the phone, Jane. The police are busy on accident calls because of the storm, and there have been a lot of victims besides ours. Better leave the phone line empty in case they want to get us. Look. Got a pencil?" I took a stub out of my bag for him and he took an old envelope out of his bathrobe pocket and printed something. He flashed the light on it for a minute and grinned as I read: "Phone Out of Order". He stood there for a minute, attaching it in some way to the phone, and then grabbed my arm and headed me toward my own room.

"Come on. I might as well begin here. We're searching the place, Jane. And you are part of the 'we.' The rest of it is Broad and me."

"But what good would I be? Besides, oughtn't somebody to go to the station and see if they'll hurry up?" I objected.

"Listen, Jane. The police are my business. I've just talked to them. They seem to think that a live accident and storm case is more important than a couple of corpses. The morgue can wait for these for a while, and the homicide squad will get here all dressed up in slickers and with little murder bags under their arms just in time to hear that Bob Riley and Jane Robbins have the murderer neatly tied up with the rope from the laundry. Are you with me on the murderer-hunt, kid?"

I had more than a slim hunch that the reason why we didn't need to hunt the murderer was that the murderer was right there, red hair and all, but it was more sensible to agree to fall in with his plans, so I said: "I'm with you," and he called into the darkness:

"Hey! Bill Broad. First floor waiting!"

And clattering down the stairs just as if the place was flooded with light came Bill Broad. I couldn't see him, but I did get a faint suggestion of whiteness that showed where his dinner jacket left off and his shirt began, so I suppose that the dawn was beginning to come, in spite of the storm.

The thunder was rumbling now instead of roaring and the lightning was going to some more appreciative globe, but the rain didn't show any signs of letting up.

My room was a dungeon, and the familiar furniture on which Riley flashed his light only made it more frightening.

They looked everywhere, behind curtains, in the cupboard, under the bed, everywhere. The only thing they saw that didn't belong there was a handful of small change, dimes and pennies and nickels flung down on the floor beside the mantel piece.

"You'd better be more careful of your pennies or they won't grow into dollars, Jane," Riley kidded me, and stopped to pick up the coins. But when he touched them he looked at me suddenly, sharply, and then I saw the light he held tremble a little as I he turned it toward the coins in his hand. Then he tucked the light under his arm, took another envelope out of the apparently inexhaustible supply of old ones in his bathrobe pocket, and slipped the coins into it, carefully sealing the envelope and writing some words on the outside before he put it back into his pocket.

When he spoke again his voice was rough and uncertain and a little of the excitement had gone out of it. "Did you drop that money on the floor, Jane?" he asked.

"Of course not," I told him. Then on impulse I added: "Listen, Riley, there was a dime in my pocket too. The bathrobe was right next to the mantelpiece on that little chair, and whoever dropped the money there must have slipped the dime in my pocket or else it fell in."

"Give me the dime," ordered Riley.

"I gave it to Mr. Broad to put into the telephone. You see he didn't have a nickel, and he wanted to call the police."

"I see," said Riley slowly, and I wanted to observe his face but couldn't. "You gave him the dime because he wanted to call the police and didn't have any change—not a nickel."

Broad said not a word. I put out my hand to feel his arm to make sure that he was still there.

He wasn't. Somewhere between the time we had come into the room and now Broad had slipped away. Riley and I were alone in the big dark room.

Then Riley flashed the light for a moment and I saw the big red splash on the white marble mantelpiece, and for a minute I was tempted to let out a shriek that would out-Dulcy Dulcy.

Because there, in my own room, on the mantelpiece that had been spotless at bedtime, was a splash of blood.

In *my* room! Blood!

4

Blood on the mantelpiece in my room.

Yet in neither of the two deaths in the house on that night of storm had I seen any blood at all.

· Blood on my bathrobe, only somehow I couldn't bring myself to tell Riley about that.

And as we stood looking at each other in the glare of light from the flash, the doorbell rang. Or was it the telephone? No. The doorbell. Neither Riley nor I moved. We heard Broad and Mrs. Meyer coming down the stairs. They opened the door, fumbling a little with the catch, and I heard somebody say:

"The police."

As if she had been waiting for her cue at the head of the stairs, Dulcy made the most of this new audience.

Her screams were as perfect as if she had rehearsed them, which of course, in a way, she had.

Riley said nothing. He clicked the electric torch and the light went off. We stood alone in the dark. For a little while we had trusted each other as a man trusts God. Now doubt had come between us, and fear. He might be the murderer. He might be a fiend who had murdered twice, maybe three times, because the blood might be the symbol of another murder.

Or he might be exactly what he seemed, a kid reporter trying to get himself a real reputation through solving a murder before the police got there.

It would take one of those explanations to make clear why he had cut the telephone wire so we couldn't reach the police—although I did think that it was a little careless of him not to test the phone, so he'd know whether the storm hadn't done his job for him.

And with the police, came the light. Ten minutes after the first policeman came into the house the lights came on. In my room there was still darkness, although the hall light was bright. In the half-light I could see Riley, poised as if to run, his red hair like the brush of a fox.

I touched the button beside me and my lights went on too.

We stood and looked at each other for a moment, like two dogs measuring each other as they circle around before a fight.

I knew that I must look a sight. After all, I had dressed in the dark. But I was at an advantage in that, because Bob Riley hadn't more than half dressed. He wore an old pair of slacks under a shabby bathrobe, and nothing else that I could see, except a pair of carpet slippers.

I had heard the police on the stairs. No. It was only one policeman. The other man who had stood outside the door had gone.

One policeman to find two murderers. No. That was silly. The law of coincidence was against that. If two people had been murdered, then it was more than likely that one person had done the two murders, although the two methods of murder were so different. There was no pattern in them at all, nothing in common, except the fact that both Henry and Miss Lizzie were extras: people who weren't important to anybody, people whom nobody loved.

Of course Dulcy was going around proclaiming her love for Henry, but I, for one, didn't believe it. Maybe I was skeptical, but a girl doesn't act for an audience when she has lost the man she really loves.

We remained in that room for ten more minutes. I went over to the corner washstand and splashed some water on my face and hands and ran a comb through my hair. Then I made the couch that was my bed, and picked up a few odds and ends that were around the room and put away some notebooks that were lying on my desk.

Twice Riley said, in a sort of tentative way, that I'd better leave things as they were for the police to examine, since the bloodstain was on the mantelpiece, but for some stubborn reason I wouldn't do this, so he just settled down in my big chair and watched me with a helpless expression in his eyes. He fumbled in the pocket of his slacks and brought out a villainous pipe and a tin of the worst tobacco I had ever smelled. He proceeded to fill the pipe in the wrong way, because how could a man smoke a pipe for a minute without knowing that if you don't put the tobacco in right the pipe won't draw right? My grandfather had explained that to me a long time ago when he taught me to fill his pipe for him. I had a package of decent tobacco, specially mixed as a Christmas gift for Bud, my big brother. I was tempted to dig it out, with the pipe that went with it, and present it to Riley, so I wouldn't have to smell the other stuff, but I'd sacrificed my small brother's gift and I didn't want to buy a whole new list of Christmas gifts.

The doorbell rang again, and this time a number of men stood on the steps. Riley opened the door, and I heard him greet one of them and usher the whole gang upstairs.

One man had, of all things, a camera. A couple of them had bags, like doctors, and only one of the bunch was in uniform. They strode up the stairs, and there I was, all alone again.

I went over to the mantelpiece and stood examining it with my hands tight behind me so I wouldn't forget and touch anything. If you're innocent you oughtn't to leave fingerprints and make people think you're a murderer, I thought, and then laughed at myself, a little grimly, for not realizing that, since this was my own room, my fingerprints were probably everywhere around, even on the mantelpiece itself.

I wasn't afraid. Having light made things seem more real again, without the fantastic nightmare quality that you get from an experience lived through in the dark.

The storm was over. The rain had stopped. I looked at my watch and saw that it was almost five o'clock and the day must be dawning behind the clouds.

Suddenly I realized that I was ravenously hungry, so I got out my little percolator and the can of coffee and went behind the screen that hid my electric plate. But I kept remembering Riley's helpless look and I wondered whether part of his attitude was due to hunger, too. I put away the little percolator and took out the big one that I have for parties, and began to spoon in enough to serve a gang.

The cream was out of a can, and the only things resembling food in the room were a box of rather stale crackers and a can of sardines, but I got those out and then went to the doorway to see if I could hail Riley and Broad.

Broad wasn't anywhere to be seen, but Riley was right there, sitting on the bottom step, watching me through the open door.

"Is that coffee for me?" he wheedled, with something of his old charm.

I nodded and answered brusquely: "If you're not afraid that it might be poison."

He smiled rather weakly. "I'd take it anyhow, provided it tasted of coffee," he said. "I'm dying for a cup. If they gave me a choice today between a byline and a cup of coffee, I'd take the coffee. Lead on, Lady Macbeth."

That was supposed to be a subtle reference, I guess, to the spot of blood on my mantlepiece, but anyhow we were at the table, drinking coffee and trying to open the can of sardines, before we said anything else about the murders.

Then Riley put down his second cup of coffee, made a last, and this time effectual stab at the sardine can, and then said:

"Little fishes in a can,

"How I wonder what you am.

"The poetry's bad, but I'm hungry enough to eat the can and all. Give me the crackers, Jane, and tell me: Do you know where Torrence lives since he left here?"

"I didn't know that he left. I did know that he got out of Betty's place when Aunt Lizzie started acting up again. But he took that little hall room on the second floor. Hasn't he still got it?" As I spoke, I kept remembering Betty's voice as she had told me that Torrence had murdered Miss Lizzie. Had she told the police, I wondered, or Riley? Or was it just one of Riley's bold guesses?

"Torry left two days ago. Betty told us that. She says that she doesn't know where he is and hasn't seen him since he left. But Mrs. Meyer saw him in the house tonight, just after eight. And Dulcy saw him after twelve, coming out of Henry's room."

"I don't believe it," I retorted as flatly as I could with my mouthful of crackers.

"Don't talk with your mouth full, little girl. You sputter," Riley said, and filled my coffee cup again companionably. "It might be a lie if it was only Dulcy, but Mrs. Meyer doesn't lie. She doesn't have to."

The remark sounded like one of those cryptic ones that men make so women will ask them questions, so I refrained pointedly from further remarks, and Riley went on:

"The thin musician who sings while she packs chocolates saw him too. Madame Terracci says that he took the box of candy and left it on Henry's table. She says it's a box that she gave to Betty last week. And she says that she's sure that it had ground glass put in it or something so that it killed 'em both, Miss Lizzie and Henry. She says that the candy was all right when she gave it to Betty, but that 'demon of murderers, Torrence' put in the ground glass and fed it to Miss Lizzie and then to Henry."

There was something especially horrible about the idea of a box of candy with ground glass in it. But Riley pointed at my coffee and shoved the can of milk at me.

"No ground glass in your coffee, kid. Drink it. You'll need it. It's a long time between drinks, said the light housekeeper in Apartment H to the light housekeeper in Apartment A. Besides, the candy gal doesn't know what she is talking about. If these people died from ground glass I'll eat this flashlight."

"Then what did they die of? And who killed them?"

"God knows. I don't. And maybe the police will."

A voice came from the doorway: "You flatter the police." The voice was as gray and colorless as the dawn that was breaking. The man who entered my room was little and sleepy and vague. He looked like a vagrant spruced up temporarily in order to coax a meal from a housewife, and the way he eyed our coffee pot and crackers was in tune with his appearance.

"Hi, Burke. I'm Riley. Remember?"

"Yeah. I remember. You asked more questions in the week you took over than the rest of the police reporters in a year. Are you as much a nuisance around the house as you are at a precinct station? This your wife?"

I didn't blush, even if Riley said afterwards that I did. "I'm Jane Robbins," I told him coldly. "I know Mr. Riley only slightly. He looked hungry and thirsty so I shared my breakfast with him."

"And have you got any more to share with me? I like my coffee lukewarm. Don't bother to heat it. No sugar, but as much milk as you have left in the can."

He possessed himself of the coffee as he spoke and took a long drink. Then he grabbed a sardine by the tail, while Riley eyed it hungrily, pulled a couple of stale crackers out of the box and settled himself for a meal.

I was tempted to talk of my prowess in tossing omelets, and of my light hand with coffee cake, but it would have been too cruel. Besides, don't the Scandinavians eat sardines for breakfast? But maybe they aren't this kind of sardines and they don't use stale crackers with them.

Five minutes later the coffee pot, the milk and sardine cans and the cracker box were all empty, although the men still looked hungry and I know that I was, myself.

If Burke was a policeman he didn't look it. I never saw a policeman that small, but maybe he just slipped in under the size limit by wearing high heels or something.

He didn't wear any uniform and I had never heard, then, of policemen in plain clothes. I didn't read as many murder stories then as I do now. After all, now, after my experience with these murders, I consider myself an expert and so I read every one that comes off the publishers' lists. But then I thought maybe he'd been asleep and hadn't had time to get into his uniform, or maybe he'd been out with his best girl and had received the message when he got home.

"Well," said Riley, "now that the commissary's empty, what are we going to have for breakfast. Murder?"

Burke nodded. "Murder. Either brand. For choice, I'll take the praying death. It's more literary. And did you pipe the garlic smell? That was a masterpiece."

Riley ventured: "With spaghetti and tomato sauce," but he looked a little green around the gills as if the combination of sardines and murder was a little too strong for him.

"Something like that. Do you know what poison smells like garlic, Riley?" Burke's voice was still sleepy, but his eyes were oddly awake under their drooping lids.

Riley shook his head. "I know what smells like bitter almonds," he said hopefully. "I thought that maybe Henry used that, in his chocolate candy, but I couldn't quite get the smell."

"Were the chocolates poisoned with bitter almonds, Riley?"

"Ask your chemist, Burke. How would I know? We talked about ground glass, but not poison. Could a poisoned chocolate really kill a man and leave him as peaceful as Henry looked?"

Burked shrugged his weary-looking shoulders. "I don't know much about corpses. All I know is how to catch the murderers when they leave a plain trail. Did you see any trail, young ones?"

"We saw blood," I told him boldly, wondering why Riley hadn't mentioned it, wondering how he had been in the same room with a big bloodstain for all this time without smelling it out. I thought that policemen were like bloodhounds, that they could smell a bloodstain a mile off.

And what was Burke doing sitting here talking to us if he was supposed to be trailing the murderer? Unless— could it be that he thought that one of us was the murderer?

I had half a suspicion that Riley knew something more than he had told, but somehow it made me mad to have somebody else suspect him too. And as for me, surely nobody would accuse me of murder on the strength of a bloodstain on white marble. After all, I hadn't known it was there either.

"Blood?" Burke straightened up quickly, but his voice remained slow and lazy and measured as if he had to pay extra for every word he used and had decided to economize.

"Blood." Riley's voice was brisk. "There's a splotch of blood on the mantelpiece and a bloodstain on Jane's bathrobe. She doesn't know anything about 'em. The spots got there without her knowledge. In the same way she knows nothing about some change that we found a little while ago, here on the floor. That was sticky with blood, too. Jane knows nothing about how the blood or the money came to be in her room."

So he knew about the spot on the bathrobe. Then why hadn't he said anything to me about it? And why hadn't he told me that there was blood on the money? And what about the dime in my pocket?

So that he'd know everything, I added quickly: "Mr. Burke, besides that money, there was a dime in my pocket, the pocket with the bloodstain. Maybe the dime had blood on it, too. But how did the dime get in my pocket? Nobody else could have worn my bathrobe. There's nobody in the house small enough except Dulcy, and she wouldn't be caught dead in anything without ruffles."

But I didn't tell him about Riley cutting the telephone wire, or ask whether Broad had really phoned him when he pretended to, or whether Riley had really talked to him or only carried on a one-sided conversation with the hook down.

"There was no blood on either of the murdered persons," Burke told us. "Is there anybody else missing from this house tonight?"

"George," I remembered.

"Torry," Riley said. "He doesn't live here, exactly, but he did until recently, and his wife is here. It is her aunt, Lizzie, who was killed. And George is one of Henry's roommates."

"Was there any connection between Miss Lizzie and Henry?" asked Burke, as if it really didn't make much difference. I bet that his casual manner got him more information in the long run than an advertising agency questionnaire.

"None at all," I said, confident that I was telling the truth.

"Then there's nothing at all, I suppose," put in Burke, "to the rumor that the reason why Dulcy refused to marry Henry was that Miss Lizzie told her some scandal in the early life of Henry?"

"You made it up," I challenged him.

Burke shook his head. "Then you probably haven't heard the rest of it either," he said gently. "You see, Henry didn't leave a suicide note, but he did leave a letter saying that he was planning to murder Miss Lizzie because she had killed every happiness that he had in the world."

"And then Henry, after killing Miss Lizzie, committed suicide?" Riley's voice was incredulous, and I felt that way too.

"No." Burked seemed regretful. "It would make a neat case that way. The only trouble is that Henry didn't kill himself. You see, Henry was murdered, and we have definite evidence that the method chosen by Henry for his murder of Miss Lizzie was not the same method used by the real murderer.

"So there is still a murderer at large," finished Riley calmly.

Burke nodded and sat back in my big chair. "Somewhere in this house," he said, "at this time, is a murderer."

5

I still didn't know, at the moment when Burke told us that there was a murderer still in the house, exactly how he had gotten all this information in such a few minutes. It couldn't have been more than half an hour between the time he went upstairs and the time he came down to join us in our ungodly breakfast. Maybe policemen can do more in half an hour than other people can in many hours. And the last ten minutes of the time he had had that gang of men with the camera and the bags to help him.

I had several new things to figure out and no time or energy to do it. Maybe I'd better be like a patient in a hospital. I remembered that time I went to have my appendix out and got into that mood of lack of responsibility for myself that is so inevitable a part of an operation. Murder must be like that, too. You have to sit back and not think or act but let the experts act and think for you.

But it is hard to do, especially when you're eighteen and ready for things to happen, even murder.

Burke ushered us upstairs. The place looked different with the lights on. Everybody was still standing around, but most of them had their clothes on now. Dulcy's three cavaliers and the little gray man from the top floor were consulting in a corner, and consulting with them was Madame Terracci, the thin elderly musician who worked in the candy factory. She was telling her theory, and the gray man was objecting more strenuously than I should have considered possible. Madame Terracci was a sweet old thing.

Burke listened to him for a few minutes, and I watched Burke and the little man and realized that there was a definite resemblance between the two. Both were little and colorless. Both had the same casual manner and toneless voice. The man's name was Smith. Or was it? Did people like that ever give their real names? Maybe he was the murderer in disguise. It would be easy enough to disguise a man who looked like that.

Wasn't it Oliver Wendell Holmes or somebody like that who wrote something like "Fate tried to conceal him by naming him Smith?" Maybe Smith had played the part of his own Fate and given himself the name.

It was at this minute that I began to look suspiciously on Smith. Madame Terracci from the candy factory seemed to regard him with hatred, as if she'd just as soon plunge an operatic dagger into his breast, because he was telling her that her theory of ground glass in the chocolates was all poppycock. "You've been seeing too many melodramas," he told her. "Candy is candy. Murder is murder. Count the simple obvious murders and then count all of those fictional-real-life things, like ground glass or poisoned chocolates, and you'll find that ninety-nine out of a hundred victims die in obvious ways and are killed by the most obvious murderers."

Burke was listening as if the idea had never occurred to him before. Smith turned around, and when he saw Burke, he flushed a little, as if the idea of being listened to by a stranger was embarrassing.

"Who're you?" Smith asked.

"Burke. Homicide squad. Want to talk to you. Where's your room?" Smith led the way and Burke followed, and we watched the two of them go off together like twins who had secrets to tell each other that they wouldn't think of telling to the common herd.

Dulcy had gotten herself dressed. She had omitted rouge and lipstick and was dressed for the occasion in a black chiffon dress, slightly ballroom, dripping with matching black lace ruffles. Her face powder was a shade too white and her hair looked like brass ringlets on a beautiful robot.

She was the dramatic young widow, touching a lace handkerchief to her eyes every two minutes. Fortunately her eyes weren't red, and the tears, so far as I could tell, were nonexistent. She was the CHIEF MOURNER with capitals.

Betty was standing in the hall outside of her room.

"Jane," she whispered, "they've chased me out. And they haven't found Torry. He went out alone before the storm, and there have been all sorts of accidents tonight, they tell me—cars derailed, and automobile accidents. The traffic's been terrible. Jane, I just know that Torry's hurt and is lying somewhere in a hospital. He wouldn't leave me this way, otherwise."

Had she completely forgotten that she had told me Torrence had murdered Miss Lizzie? Or didn't she dare confess it even to herself for fear that a policeman would read her mind? I could understand that. If I had been in Betty's place I'd probably have felt that way myself.

She was looking even more fragile than usual, with her face innocent of any makeup. But she didn't dramatize the situation the way Dulcy did. She had put on a plain crisp cotton house dress, and her hair was neatly combed and pinned back. She looked young and pretty and tired, like a child who has been up too late the night before, but who has decided to be good anyhow.

About this time the men started to come out of her room. Through the open door I could see one man folding

up a camera and another packing some other things neatly in a bag. There was a circle in chalk drawn around the
place where Miss Lizzie had been, and Miss Lizzie herself
was nowhere to be seen. Later, when the men came downstairs carrying what might have been two big baskets or
hampers, I realized that the bodies had been taken away
for further examination, but I didn't see any of the details
that are inevitable in this type of murder.

Later, when I asked questions, Burke showed me all of
the contents of one of those murder bags that Riley had
talked about, and told me all of the facts about the finger-
printing, photographing and measurement that the police
went through in every case of mysterious murder, but at
that time everything seemed as mysterious as diplomacy
to me.

I made some more coffee as soon as I got Betty down
into my room. She had to drink it black and without even
crackers and sardines as accompaniment, because Burke
and Riley had finished up everything in sight, but when I
saw a little color coming into her face I knew that black
coffee had its uses, although it might taste like nothing in
civilization. I belong to the cream brigade of coffee drink-
ers, myself. There wasn't time for biscuits or a cake.

Betty seemed to want to talk, so I let her, hoping that
Burke wasn't hiding in the woodwork taking notes.

"Jane," she said, "I've been thinking about the day my
baby died. Did you ever know exactly what happened?
Aunt Lizzie killed my baby, deliberately killed him. He
had a high fever with a cold, and when I left the room
for a minute she took him out and had him prayed over
by one of those funny sects of hers, and by the time they
had finished handling him out in the cold and the rain he
had pneumonia, and he died. Torrence wanted to tell the
police and make them arrest her, but she's an old woman
and I felt sorry for her because I thought she had tried to

do her best for the baby. But Torry was right, Jane. We should have told the police then. And this would never have happened, and Torry would never have killed Aunt Lizzie."

"Don't say it, Betty," I whispered. "Don't even think it. Surely Torry didn't kill Aunt Lizzie, and certainly he didn't kill Henry. Why should Torry want to kill Henry?"

"I don't know about Henry. Maybe Henry just died. Maybe he had heart trouble."

"The kind of heart trouble Henry had," I said grimly, "you spell with a capital D. And D is for Dulcy. Henry was murdered. And it's likely that the person who murdered Henry murdered Miss Lizzie too. So you see," I finished triumphantly, "since it's impossible for Torry to have murdered Henry, then it's unlikely that he murdered anybody at all, including Miss Lizzie."

For the first time Betty came alive. "Jane"—her voice was almost a whisper—"do you think that he didn't do it? Could he have gone away before somebody else came to murder her? And who was it? Who could have killed her?"

"Almost anybody," I suggested recklessly, exhilarated by the sight of Betty's hope. "Smith could have done both murders. Look how unlikely a person he is. Did you ever hear him talk before? Neither did I. And the only thing that excites him enough to make him talk is murder. So look, Betty, isn't he the likely person to have done the murders? Burke must have thought so too, because look how Burke took him in a corner to talk to him right away."

I didn't believe the theories I advanced, not exactly. I was still thinking of Broad and of Riley, of their monkeyshines with the telephone and of their odd behavior from time to time during the evening. Look at the way that Broad had disappeared when we found the bloodstained money, and how quickly he had appeared with Mrs. Meyer later, from upstairs.

"And there's Mrs. Meyer," Betty offered quickly, building a foundation of hope for herself, for Torry. "She's the sort of person who might murder if she didn't get what she wanted. She's a strange person, one of a kind. And she's beautiful, and we don't any of us know where she came from or who are her friends. Maybe she's a part of Henry's past, and she's the one that Miss Lizzie found out about and told Dulcy about, or threatened to. Did she ever really tell Dulcy, Jane?"

"I don't know whether she mentioned names, Betty. But I do know that Henry left a letter saying that she had ruined every chance for happiness he had and that he planned to murder her."

"Then it's murder and suicide." Betty looked so happy that I hated to dispel her hopes.

"Burke says not," I told her flatly. "Henry was killed too. And Miss Lizzie died in an entirely different way from the one that Henry mentioned in his letter."

"Maybe he changed his mind about the way, and then somebody came along—and murdered him too. Or maybe his death was an accident that looked like murder."

But Betty faltered a little, and I could see that she didn't believe her brave remarks. She shivered, and I realized that it was cold in the big room.

These houses that are relics of past glory aren't so easy to heat as modern apartment houses. I went to the wardrobe to get her something to throw over her shoulders—a coat, or maybe my bathrobe. And as I thought of the bathrobe, I remembered the blood on the pocket and hastily scrambled through the clothes to see where the robe was.

I looked, and looked again.

The bathrobe was gone. Bloodspot and all, it was gone. I took the jacket of my suit to Betty, and then, while she was putting it on, I took a look at the mantlepiece. The spot was still there. But on the rest of the mantlepiece there was some sort of a yellowish powder.

I hadn't an idea why it was there. As a matter of fact, I had some feeling that it might be something poisonous put there for added murderous purposes.

It wasn't until later, when Burke explained, that I knew what it was.

I had a queer taste in my mouth from the sardines and the black coffee, and so I thought that I could puzzle out the happenings just as well while I brushed my teeth. I went behind the screen that sheltered my washbasin, and reached for the glass. But sometime between five o'clock and then my glass had disappeared. And until I heard Burke's explanation later, I didn't see the connection between the disappearance of my glass and the powder on the mantlepiece.

At the time it was just one more thing to wonder about.

"Betty," I asked uneasily, "was Madame Terracci telling the truth about that candy? Did she give it to you?"

Betty nodded. My jacket was a little tight for her, so she just put it across her shoulders to take off the chill. "Madame Terracci always brings me candy. They make it there where she works. I don't care much about chocolates, but she wants to be friendly, and Torry likes them, so I let her give them to me. Then I send her soup or pot roast when I fix it, and we're all even. They—they didn't really discover that there was anything wrong with the chocolates, did they, Jane?"

I didn't know, of course, and there didn't seem to be any way of finding out. It was just at that time I looked out of the room and saw some of the police leaving, and it must have been then that they took the two bodies away.

People were moving around in the hall, peering in through the half open door, until finally I closed it and came back in to lounge on the couch that was my bed.

I was suddenly terribly tired. The fear had all worn away with this excitement. Now that Betty was here with me, something of her worry for Torry transferred itself to me, and I kept wondering how he had killed Miss Lizzie, if he had killed her, and why he had killed Henry, if he had killed him.

I could understand the motive for killing Miss Lizzie, but not the method, and neither the motive nor the method for Henry's murder was clear at all.

But then I wasn't an expert. I didn't know much about anything except the office where I worked and the small town I came from and the way people acted at home when tragedy came to their families. There was neighborliness there, and not this suspicion that seemed to cast a spell over the whole house.

My robe with the bloodspot. My mantel with the bloodstain. My glass gone. The bloody money on my floor. The mystery about the telephone. Suspicious things, all of them.

And in all the house there was only one person of whose innocence I was assured. That was Betty, Torry's wife, who sat there in my chilly room, with my jacket over her slim shoulders.

But she—did she trust me, too? Was she as sure of my innocence as I was of hers?

With a sudden realization of what I must seem to those around me, I made up my mind about that. I, who was innocent, looked more guilty than most of the rest of them. If I had seen anybody else with such a damning collection of bloodstains, my trust for her would have been non-existent.

Therefore how could I, with any hope that my ideas might be true, build a case against any of these others who must be building the same kind of case against me?

I was like the old lady who woke up to find her petticoats cut and who went around saying: "This is never I." Because murder suspects were different kinds of people, not just regular ordinary people like me. Not eighteen-year-old girls with jobs as stenographers, with a suit and three dresses for every day, one evening dress and a Sunday-go-to-meeting dress-up dress. Not girls who budgeted their small salaries in order to get enough cash for Christmas and birthday presents for their families back home. In short, suspects were other folks—not me.

But with the memory of Burke's watchful eyes I knew, at that moment, that of all the people in the house that night, my own actions had been most suspicious.

As calmly as possible I took cigarettes and matches from the table to Betty, lit a cigarette for her and one for myself, and then went back to the couch and propped myself up with a couple of pillows. Luckily I wouldn't have to go to work today.

"There's the other couch over there, Betty, if you want to be lazy," I told her, but she shook her head.

"I want to sit up," she said. "It makes me feel ready to go and do something if Torry comes and I need to do anything for him." I couldn't quite understand that, but she seemed comfortable, so I let it go at that.

We were still sitting there smoking, without saying anything at all important, when Burke opened the door and came in.

He went right over to the table, picked up a cup and poured himself some coffee. "It's lukewarm, the way I like it," he said, "and I guess there isn't any more cream, so I'll drink it this way."

"Well," he said finally, after he had finished one cup and taken another, "Mr. Smith has an idea. He seems to think that you, Miss Jane, killed Miss Lizzie, to save Mrs. Betty here. Then Henry came along and saw you and you had to kill him to keep him from giving the alarm. Riley is helping you, he thinks. In fact he goes so far as to say that Riley cut the telephone wire to keep a message from reaching the police. He says that he saw Riley cutting the wire and that he saw a bloodstain on your robe and he wouldn't be surprised if you had killed George too and hidden the body somewhere in this room. Too bad that you haven't more sardines with this coffee, Miss Jane. I kind of relish sardines with black coffee."

"So I was considering earlier, Mr. Burke," I told him frankly. "I figured that there was more evidence against me than anybody else. The only thing is that I didn't do the murders and don't know who did."

"Where would you put the body if you had killed George? Any cupboards big enough for corpses—or skeletons? Any porches?"

"You've looked in my cupboards?"

Burke put down his cup again and nodded. "And found a bloodstained bathrobe," he said. "You don't know anything about the bloodstains. Any porches? What about that little balcony outside the window?"

"Nothing on that more dangerous than a rubber tree," I told him. "Look, if you want to."

He did. He opened the window and the chill air poured in. After the night of storm the morning was breaking. The dark clouds were turning rosy now, and there was a hint of sunrise at the horizon.

And on the little balcony, soggy wet, quiet as death, was the crumpled figure of a man.

I could hear Betty's sharp breath. "Torry. Torry." It was almost a whisper. And swiftly, she sped past both of us and was down on her knees beside the figure. Torry had come home.

6

We had Torry off of the balcony and on my bed faster than it takes to tell it. I had an old rubberized sheet that I had used in my Camp Fire Girl days, and that saved the blankets. Betty didn't waste any time in tears or screams or hysterics.

He was breathing, and that was about all. There was a streak of blood down his cheek, and his hand was bleeding. At some time he had had his bleeding hand in his pocket, because there was a little blood in the pocket and on the money, and when he saw the blurred brown stains on the change that was in Torry's pocket, Burke turned a curious glance at me. I could just see him weighing the possibility of whether my five feet nothing could sock a six foot man into unconsciousness and then put him on the balcony outside my window.

We made him dry and as comfortable as possible, and then Burke went out to call a doctor. Yes, the telephone was working now, although the "out of order" sign that Riley had put on it was still there.

"Doc," Burke said into the phone, "I've got objections to you getting to bed again while I've got to stay up. Slip a cup of coffee and a couple of doughnuts in your pocket for me and come on back to the light housekeeping place.

Yes. Another one. Not a murder this time, though. Looks like concussion, but you can't tell."

Torry hadn't opened his eyes, and so far as I could see, hadn't regained consciousness, but he seemed more comfortable, and at least she had him with her now, so Betty wasn't quite so frightened. She just sat there holding the hand on which she had put iodine and a bandage from my first aid kit, and the expression on her face was more peaceful than I had ever seen it.

She had Torry and she wasn't looking any further ahead than that.

When the doctor got there it was one of the men who had come before. He looked tired and sleepy, but he had really stopped to get some doughnuts and a paper cup of coffee for Burke, who sat himself down at my table and engulfed the coffee and doughnuts. He offered us some, but when we refused he just went on eating and drinking with some of the placidity of the girl who went on cutting bread and butter. That was in Goethe or Schiller or somebody like that.

At any rate the doctor didn't seem to be much worried. He told Betty that Torry would probably sleep for most of the next twenty-four hours and might wake up entirely all right. He left some sort of medicine in case Torry woke up later, and said to call him if there seemed to be any change.

Burke suggested that a hospital might be a good bet, but Torry's wife shook her head. "I'll take care of him," she said. "He's all I have now."

Even Burke didn't have nerve enough to suggest at this point that if Torry was the murderer he wouldn't be there much longer for Betty to take care of.

"We'll post a guard outside the door here," Burke said, and I wasn't any too sure that he meant the guard to protect us. Maybe he meant to protect the rest of the household from us.

Betty went upstairs and came back bringing things that she and Torry needed. Riley helped her carry the stuff down, and Burke and the doctor stood there, in my room, watching Torry while Betty was gone.

Burke said, in that casual way of his: "Going to stay here, too? I see that there are two beds. Or shall we get a stretcher and carry him upstairs to his own room? The body's been moved out. The room is open again."

The doctor shook his head. "Better not move him. Let him stay here. I'd insist on a hospital, but they're pretty full, what with all the traffic accidents tonight, and that streetcar crash. His wife will take care of him, and this girl here looks like she could help."

"Yeah," Burke said meaningly, "she could help." He took a look at the place on the mantel where the blood was, and I wondered whether he was being subtle again and suggesting that I was the cause of Torry's present troubles.

After the doctor left, Betty settled Torry on the couch-bed with herself in the big chair beside him where his eyes would fall on her when he awoke. I took the other couch and spent at least a couple of hours napping, with one ear half-cocked for the excitement that didn't come. The house was quiet, as if everybody else were napping too. We heard people going up and down the stairs, and once in a while I heard footsteps outside the door as if somebody intended to knock. But nobody did, and eventually I awoke from my nap and began to feel civilized again.

I went out into the hall with my bath basket and clean clothes and managed to find the first-floor bathroom empty. My bath was hot and refreshing, and I went back into my room feeling like a million. Betty was asleep and Torry seemed unconscious, but there was a sort of pathetic helpless expression on his face, like that of a child asleep in a strange place. Betty looked frightened even in her sleep, and she held tight to Torry's hand as if she were afraid that somebody would take him away from her.

I slipped out of the door again, closing it carefully behind me, and went to stand on the doorstep and look out toward the street. I was startled to realize that there was a cluster of flowers on the door, tied with crepe ribbons.

The conventional symbol of death, as put up by a cheap but respectable undertaker. No, they called them morticians now. But they still put flowers of death on the door to point out that one more body would lie at rest.

There were two deaths but only one cluster of purple flowers. Odd.

The morning was advanced so that the sun was high in the sky. The air blew fresh and brisk, and tossed my hair around my face. It was hard to believe that murder could come on a day like this. Last night the storm had made murder seem almost natural. But surely nothing could die on a day that looked so alive.

I sat down on the stoop outside and tried to figure out exactly what I should do.

I didn't have to go to the office. My boss was away at a convention and he had given me Thursday and Friday off.

"Jane Robbins," he had said, "you take these two days and this extra check and you paint the town red while I'm gone. I intend to paint Chicago red while I'm there, and you'll keep the color scheme even." The check had been for an extra week's salary, which accounted for the fact that I wanted to be up and out, in spite of the murders. Hunt's were having a half-price sale on hats, and they had a silly topknot that consisted of a ribbon, a garland of flowers and a piece of felt. It sounds terrible, but I adored it, and when it got down to my financial reach, I wanted it. Today was the day, with that extra salary in my purse, and it was up to me to persuade Burke that I didn't have a thing to do with those murders.

While I was missing, Dulcy's shriek broke through the morning sunshine as it had broken through last night's storm.

She might have been screaming about anything from a mouse to another murder, and there wasn't much that I could do about any of these troubles, so I just sat where I was for a while longer, while Dulcy went on screaming.

Finally I had to go and see what was happening, so I gave one last look at the sun and went into the house. Dulcy was standing at the top of the stairs, dressed in a black suit with touches of crisp white. She looked like a young widow, ready to put on her hat and gloves for a visit to her lawyer's office to hear about her late husband's investments. The only thing that spoiled it was the red paint-on fingernails that looked incredibly long and sharp.

She was grabbing at the stair-rail and letting one shriek after another come from that carefully crimsoned mouth.

Riley was standing on one side of her and Burke on the other and both of them were trying to hear what she was shrieking about.

But when she saw me she stopped shrieking and pointed, and as she pointed she called: "There she is. There—she—is." And she went off in one of those dying calf moans that sound like something out of an Irish banshee tale.

Burke and Riley let go Dulcy so quickly that she had to grab at the railing again to keep from falling. Then they ran down the steps two steps at a time, and I remember thinking that it was lucky that Burke wasn't as big as Riley or the two of them would have got wedged in the stairway, shoulder to shoulder.

It looked funny to see the two of them advancing on me, down the stairs, and I couldn't help the trace of a grin in spite of the horror of the whole business. Because when something is as terrible as murder, you just can't take it in your stride, and so you keep your mind on little unimportant things.

I remember the time I broke my ankle at basketball. I can remember every word of a silly masquerade ball poster that was pinned to the bulletin board right behind the school doctor's desk. All the time they were fixing my ankle, I kept looking at it so I wouldn't be a coward and cry. For years afterward, I could have quoted every word of that poster and even drawn the foolish cartoons at the top of the page, and I'm no artist, I assure you. Yet I don't remember the pain of the ankle at all.

This was something of the same kind. I knew that something had happened to make Dulcy point at me with that shrieking horror. But since I couldn't see what she could blame me for, I could only chuckle at the funny sight of the men coming down the stairs toward me.

Both got to me at the same moment. They grabbed my arms as if they expected me to run away.

Burke said, a little breathless, but still casual, "Weren't running away, were you? Not now."

I felt a little blank. I hadn't gone anywhere or done anything. "I've just been sitting on the doorstep looking at the weather," I told them. "What's all the shooting for?"

"Not shooting," answered Burke dryly. "But murder, nevertheless."

"You don't mean—more—"

"Yes, Miss Jane. More murder."

Madly my thoughts darted from one to another of those remaining. "Not Torry? Or George?"

Riley said: "See, Burke. I told you she didn't know. She doesn't even know who it is."

"Says you. The chocolates are to blame again, Miss Jane."

"Not—ground glass," I was horrified, remembering how Riley and I had hooted at the fantastic idea of Madame Terracci: that ground glass had been put in the candy and had caused the death.

I looked at Riley, and he was looking at me, and I could see that he was remembering too.

"It was the music teacher, Madame Terracci," Burke told me, and this time I felt a pang of regret.

So far as I knew she had never been anything but kind and friendly. She had brought chocolates to Betty, because she felt sorry for her, because she could see Betty's unhappiness and hoped to assuage it a little.

Henry and Miss Lizzie hadn't seemed important to me, and their deaths had seemed horrible but unreal. Here, for the first time, there was unhappiness in the idea of this death.

I knew that my eyes were full of tears and I couldn't help swallowing hard as I turned to Burke. "I'm sorry. I hope it didn't—didn't hurt her. Did she die as terribly as the others? And do you know who did it?"

"Dulcy says"—Burke's voice was casual—"that you did."

It was a shock, like a needle going straight into your hand when you're sewing. "But, Mr. Burke—you know I couldn't—I didn't."

"I know you say you couldn't—you didn't."

"Do you believe Dulcy and not me?" Somehow it didn't occur to me that anybody could believe Dulcy, who told lies straight along, and not believe me. It seemed, if anything, more unjust than being accused of murder.

Riley said: "I believe you. If it had been anybody else, I mightn't. But you liked that old girl. I've seen you taking up coffee to her when she came home too tired to go out. And I know you've asked her to sing for you because she loved to sing for an audience, although her voice is pretty bad now. A gal doesn't murder anybody she likes that much."

I was touched that he had even noticed these little things. After all, they were true, and I had liked her.

And now she was dead, too. Now another purple cluster of flowers would be tied to the door to tell the street of her death.

"She left a will," Burke said gently, "and she left most of her worldly possessions to you, Miss Jane."

"No. No." I didn't want the poor woman's pitiful possessions. "The poor thing. Didn't she have any family or any friends?"

"But she wasn't poor," Burke said, still calmly. "That's the point. She wasn't poor, Miss Jane. And she left to you almost everything she owned."

"But if she wasn't poor, why did she live here? We're all poor here, Mr. Burke—Riley and Dulcy and I, and all the rest of them. We make a little and we spend a little, and our rents have to be cheap. We have little housekeeping apartments made out of ordinary lodging house rooms. We cook our meals on little stoves. We go to market to buy our vegetables cheap. We make our own clothes. No. She couldn't have been rich if she lived here, Mr. Burke." I had to make him believe me.

Riley put a hand on my arm. "You really believe that," he said. "But Burke's right. She hadn't much regular money. But she had jewels worth thousands, and bonds and real estate. It's all yours, Jane, because you were the only one of us who was kind to her except Betty. She left something to Betty, but most of her estate she left to you, Jane."

It was impossible to take it in. I wanted money—what eighteen-year-old doesn't? But I wanted to make it for myself, not to have it come to me through the death of a kindly inoffensive old girl like the musician who worked in the chocolate factory.

That reminded me. "But if she was rich, why did she work at the chocolate factory?"

Burke shrugged his shoulders. "Don't ask me. But she did work there. And the chocolate that killed her (if it did) and the chocolate that killed Henry came from a box that was made in the factory where she worked. It's the same poison, anyhow."

"But why did Dulcy say that I did it?"

"Because Dulcy says—Dulcy swears—that she saw you going down the hall and up the stairs to Madame Terracci's room with a box of candy in your hand, and she accuses you of murder to get your hands on the money she was leaving you."

"But I didn't know she was leaving me anything. And I didn't go upstairs. And I haven't had a box of candy in my hands for a year."

"Then," went on Burke, "Dulcy says that you fled from the house and came back only a few minutes ago, after having accomplished an errand of your own that had something to do with the murders."

"But I haven't been away from the house. I was sitting on the stoop outside the door. You can't believe all this of me, Mr. Burke. Tell him, Bob Riley. I'm not like that. Tell him."

As obediently as a small boy following his teacher's instructions, Riley said: "Burke, she couldn't have done it. You don't really think she did, do you? Dulcy's lying. Dulcy always lies."

"And does Mr. Smith lie, too? Because Mr. Smith says he saw Miss Jane come out of her room with the candy box in her hand and go along the hall. He didn't see her go up the stairs, but is sure that she did, even if he didn't see or hear her himself. And as evidence he offered this, that belongs, I think, to you."

On the palm of Burke's hand was a button of old silver filigree, and when I saw it I looked down at my dress. Because only last week I had found a whole set of old buttons in an antique shop. I had cleaned them up and sewed them to my black dress. And as I looked down, I saw that one button was missing. The thread was hanging loose.

I held out my hand for it, but Burke shook his head and put the button back into his pocket. "Not today," he said. "Because you see, Miss Jane, we found this button in a most incriminating place."

"Where?"

"In Madame Terracci's room, on the table, under the box of chocolates."

7

I had always thought that the first thing they did with any murder suspect was to toss him into a jail. I kept seeing bars in front of my eyes, and the shudders that ran up and down my back under the neat dark dress with the missing filigree button were only infants compared with what I expected later in the day. But surely people like me didn't go to jail.

The room that they chose for some further questioning was as far from a jail as possible. It belonged to Madame Terracci, and it was a kitchen, a neat bright kitchen, with the sunshine streaming in the yellow-curtained window. The icebox was shining, the stove was bigger than most others in the house. There was a pancake grill on the burner and a bowl of pancake batter on the table.

The pot of red jam on the table was one that I had given Madame Terracci myself. My small-town training made jam making almost second nature to me, and I was always giving jars of jam and jelly and preserves to the rest of the folks in the house. I could see my own typed labels on the jar: "Strawberry Jam." I thought of the early spring morning when I had made that jam and I wondered why I hadn't had some sort of premonition, when I typed that label, where I would next see it.

"Sit down," suggested Burke.

I sat. Riley was gone. There was a young policeman
with, of all things, a stenographer's notebook and curly
blond hair.

Burke's voice was still casual: "Got to ask you some
questions, Miss Jane. I can use the answers against you, if
there's anything in 'em to use. Understand that?"

"But there isn't anything—I mean—I understand, but
I didn't do it, Mr. Burke. I liked her. Honestly I did. And
you don't kill people you like."

"You'd be surprised, little girl, how often folks kill
folks they once loved. Do you like pancakes?"

"Yes." My eyes were on the batter from which Madame
Terracci had apparently made pancakes. But the batter was
wrong, somehow. I was cook enough to see that. I got up
and walked over to the stove and fiddled with the pancake
griddle.

I expected to have Mr. Burke tell me not to touch anything, but he didn't. He said: "What—"

The rising excitement that I couldn't conceal brought
Burke over beside the stove with me. "Look, Mr. Burke.
This is a plant. Madame Terracci wasn't making pancakes
for breakfast this morning. I'm sure of that. Somebody
wants you to think that she was. But she wasn't."

"Why?" If you can imagine a dog's casual bark, that was
Burke's voice.

"Because Madame Terracci makes thin pancakes.
Around the edge, they're like lace. And this pancake batter would make those thick things that never get cooked
clear through. And there are lumps of flour in this batter.
Madame Terracci made pancake batter like thick cream
without a single lump of any kind in it. Madame Terracci
didn't make this batter, but for some reason the murderer
wants you to think that she did. I don't know anything about
the murder except what you've told me. But I do think
that the making of pancakes has something to do with it."

The air in the room was different. The very jam seemed to glow with a new brilliance. "Could I touch this, to find out something?" I asked, motioning toward the jar. "It would have my fingerprints on it, anyhow. I made it."

"We didn't know you made it. But we knew about your fingerprints."

"How? You never took my fingerprints, Mr. Burke."

"But I did. From a glass in your room. We took it for testing when we fingerprinted your room to see who had been there. But, Miss Jane, you must be a bad housekeeper. Every person in the house has been in the room recently. It was a forest of fingerprints."

"I had a party the other night. Everybody came in for coffee and cookies. I felt lonesome and decided that I'd be neighborly even if I didn't know my neighbors well. And I guess the fingerprints got there then. I don't spend much time on housekeeping except over the week-ends. I have a job every day."

"Why aren't you on the job now, Miss Jane?"

"Well, Mr. Burke, my boss went away, and he gave me a couple of days' vacation and some extra salary, and I was supposed to paint the town red while he was gone."

I was only telling the truth, and there wasn't any reason for the kid policeman in the corner to laugh out loud and for Burke to grin. Burke said: "Somebody certainly painted this house red. Three deaths in a day—maybe four."

"Will Torry die?" I felt stricken that I hadn't even thought of Betty through all this.

A few minutes before, when the policeman in the corner had laughed, I had looked over at him and realized that he had been taking down in shorthand everything that was said. I didn't know his system and I wasn't close enough to see it clearly, anyhow, but somehow that frightened me terribly, even though I knew I hadn't anything to hide.

This pancake business was odd. I couldn't see how it would fit into a murder case, but surely it did, somehow.

I took up the jar of jam and opened the cover. The paraffine had been all broken when a couple of spoonfuls of the jam had been taken out, and that was strange, because Madame Terracci knew how to open my jams. I'd explained to her the first time I gave her a jar.

"Madame Terracci didn't open this, Mr. Burke. Somebody else did. This is a prop, too, like the pancake batter. I know it."

"How do you know it, Miss Jane?" That casual tone was maddening.

"You see this string across the top of the paraffine, Mr. Burke? I always put my paraffine in that way, and Madame Terracci knew why. Because if you take hold of the string at each end—this way—you can pull out the paraffine without breaking it to pieces. And the person who took it out didn't know this, but Madame Terracci did." These two bits of information that I had garnered from my sight of the kitchen seemed terribly important to me—more important than the evidence against me, somehow. But did they believe me? Or did they think that this was just some trick of mine to pull their attention away from the evidence of the filigree button and the lies of Dulcy and Mr. Smith?

I went closer to the stove and looked at the pancake griddle. And at what I saw, my heart went down into my heels. Because on the griddle was a lacy corner of crisp pancake. Just a sliver of it, crisp and dark brown, exactly the way Madame Terracci made her pancakes. I couldn't understand it. I simply could not reconcile it with the stiff pancake batter that would never have made thin pancakes with crisp edges, or with the paraffine all broken to bits on the top of the strawberry jam.

"What's the matter, Miss Jane? More pancake trouble?"

"Yes. Madame Terracci did make pancakes. But not from this batter. And she didn't open this jam—I know that—or mix this batter. But she did make pancakes this morning. At least she made one pancake. That's the clue, Mr. Burke. She made one little pancake for herself—early. And then somebody wanted it to look as if she had made a lot of pancakes, as if she had had company for breakfast. And since whoever it was left a button of mine on the table under a box of candy, I think that he wanted it to be thought that I had been her guest for breakfast."

It seemed so simple to me, and yet it didn't impress these men at all. They just sat like two sticks in their corners, and Burke went on: "Miss Jane, I want to ask you several things. First: Who are you? I've seen you around here for hours, and I don't really know anything about you except that you are eighteen and tiny and pretty, that you make jam and coffee and know something about cooking. You have a job with a generous boss who gives days off with extra pay instead of docking you for the days off the way that most bosses do. You live in apartment A and have a marble mantelpiece with bloodstains on it. There is evidence pointing to you as a murderess. Now tell me more about yourself, Miss Jane Robbins."

"There isn't anything much more. I have lived here in the house ever since I have been in the city—six months. I have tried to be neighborly with these people the way we are at home, in Bridgeport. But they look on me as a curiosity. I'm little, so they think I'm a child. But I'm eighteen."

"How well did you know Henry Elend?"

"He came to my parties, but he always brought Dulcy. He loved her. I never knew him well. We never talked together. Ask Dulcy about him. She'll tell lies, because she's the kind of girl who can't help dramatizing herself, but you can sift the truth from the lies."

"And you don't lie, Jane Robbins?"

"No, Mr. Burke. I don't lie. And I tell you today that I know nothing about these murders."

I think that he believed me, strangely enough. Then, for no reason at all, I began to think of Bill Broad as he had stood there on the doorstep the night before, with the storm like a backdrop behind him, and the rain just starting.

"Bill Broad knows something," I guessed, "although what it is, I don't know. He and Mrs. Meyer both know something—the same thing. I saw the way they looked at each other behind Riley's back last night when he asked if there was any connection between Henry and Miss Lizzie. And then they looked at Madame Terracci and Mr. Smith—both of them, at once. I haven't thought about it from that moment till this."

"Tell me," said Burke, "exactly what you did last night after twelve—every single thing."

"At twelve I had been in bed for two hours," I said, "and asleep, at that. Somewhere around two-thirty, and I can't tell you any closer than that, I opened the door for Bill Broad who had forgotten his key."

"The storm had started then? It was raining?"

"There was wind and thunder and lightning. But the rain was just starting."

"Was Bill Broad wet from the rain? Blown about by the wind?

"I—I don't know." I tried to remember, but I couldn't. "I felt dampness once when I touched his sleeve, but I don't remember anything else. I was too sleepy and there wasn't much light."

"Miss Jane, when you got up to open the door for Broad was the bloodstain on your mantelpiece? And did you see the stain on your robe?"

"It may have been there on the mantelpiece—that stain, I mean. I didn't turn on the light."

"Why not?"

"No special reason. Yes, there was, too. I've opened the door for people other times, and when I turn on the light in between I find it harder to go back to sleep again. So I got up in the dark and went to the door."

"Weren't you afraid, Miss Jane?"

"What was there to be afraid about? I live in a first-floor apartment and the landlady is deaf and a lot of people forget their keys, and so I guess I'm fated to be the one to open the door to them. I'm used to it."

"What time did you say this was, Miss Jane?"

"About two-thirty, I guess. I don't know. It wasn't until hours later that I actually saw a watch. It might have been any time after midnight."

"The storm was at its worst when the lights went out?"

"Yes. But that was later. By that time we knew that both Henry and Miss Lizzie were dead. And—listen, Mr. Burke, did anybody tell you about seeing ghosts? Both Mrs. Meyer and Dulcy thought that they saw Henry, just before the candles went out. Mrs. Meyer fainted and Dulcy screamed—as usual. Did they tell you, Mr. Burke?"

The memory of the terror of that moment came over me again and I closed my eyes. For one minute, I remembered, I had been doubtful about Henry's death. I had considered that Riley and Broad were in this together and that they had lied about Henry's death. I told this to Burke, and he shook his head.

"The boy was dead by one o'clock," he said, "or two at the latest. And Miss Lizzie died, they think, about twelve-thirty. Phosphorus."

"What do you mean, phosphorous?"

"I mean that they seem to think that the poison used for Miss Lizzie was some kind of mixture with phosphorous in it. That's why we got that luminous haze, and the smell like garlic."

"Then it wasn't somebody who had been eating spaghetti and tomato sauce at Tony's." I remembered Riley's comment, and thought that it would be a long time before I'd want to use garlic in my cooking again. Not after this.

Burke looked casual but patient, like a sensible maid listening to a fluttery housewife giving advice, but when I had finished he said: "You have enemies. Smith. Dulcy. Dulcy's boy-friends on the top floor. Why?"

It's a strange and startling thing to discover that you have enemies. If anybody had said to me the day before: "Jane, who are your enemies?" I'd have laughed and said: "I haven't an enemy in the world."

Now things were different. I had enemies. Enemies are people who hate you and want to get you into trouble. Enemies tell lies about you. Enemies even murder you. Miss Lizzie and Henry had had enemies. Even Madame Terracci had had enemies. And today they were dead, all three of them. I had enemies. Did that mean death for me, too? By tomorrow, would Jane Robbins mean a crepe on a door and not an alive girl of eighteen who was waiting for real life to begin, who loved to cook and to sew and be neighborly?

I felt as tied up as a muzzled dog. The first time that you realize that the world isn't full of people who want to be friends as soon as they know you is pretty terrible.

So I had enemies. Why? I said the word out loud to Burke: "Why? Why are they my enemies? I didn't do anything to them. I've never even said anything to them. I haven't talked to any of them for ten minutes."

"That's the trouble. You bothered to be friendly with Madame Terracci because you thought she was interesting. But you didn't ever notice Mrs. Meyer. You were neighborly to Betty, Torrence's wife. But you ignored Dulcy. You let young Riley tell you about the newspaper business

and young Broad talk about department stores, but you
didn't even ask questions about the young German and the
handsome Basque boy with the limp. You asked them to
your parties because everybody came. But you didn't say
two words to them except to ask them if they'd have more
coffee."

"Yes. But why should they care, Mr. Burke? I'm not important. I'm just a small-town girl in the city. Why should
they care whether I paid any attention to them?"

Burke shrugged his shoulders. "I don't know. You're
little and pretty and you mothered some of the folks in
the house. Maybe they were lonesome and wanted to be
mothered, too, even if it was a kid like you who did the
mothering. And Smith—did you ever hear about his year
as a detective?"

"No. But, Mr. Burke, he looks like you. If policemen
had understudies like movie stars, he could be yours."

Burke hummed something that turned out to be a song
of several years before. "ME AND MY SHADOW" was the
name of it, Riley told me later when I hummed it for him
and asked what it was.

"That's an idea, Miss Jane. I'll take him on the next
time I need an understudy," he said. "And, Miss Jane,
why didn't you tell me that Torrence was attacked in your
room and that you dragged him out on the balcony outside
of your window? Was it Riley who helped you? And how
did you escape the guard this morning when you left the
house?"

"But I didn't attack Torry. And I didn't leave the house.
And I didn't escape the guard. There wasn't any guard."

"There was a guard. Here he is, putting down your
words in that notebook." The curly-headed policeman
blushed and looked a little self-conscious, even guilty.
I remembered hearing Dulcy talking to somebody at the

head of the stairs when I'd gone to take a bath that morning, and I turned to the young man, who didn't seem much
older than myself—or Dulcy.

"Curly," I said coaxingly, "Let's keep it a secret that
you left the door unguarded and went up the steps to listen to Dulcy's blandishments. Didn't she call you? And
didn't you go up for just a minute?"

Curly almost stuttered, but I knew I'd hit the nail on
the head. Dulcy, again. Burke said: "Off the record, kid.
Did you leave?"

Curly nodded, redder than the potholder beside the
stove.

"And in the few minutes when you went out of the door
and this young Eagle-eye left his post, anybody could have
gone up the backstairs to Madame's room. Where were
you, Jane Robbins?"

"A girl has to bathe. After all, you wouldn't like to
see me in jail with a dirty neck," I dared to say, and he
grinned and put out his hand with a helpless gesture.

"A girl takes a bath, another girl talks to a curly-headed
policeman," he said, "and a woman gets murdered—all at
one and the same time."

8

It seemed incredible that there should have been such a short margin of time between life and death. Between safety because a guard stood at a door at the foot of a flight of stairs, and danger because a couple of doors were left unguarded so that somebody could have come in and gone up the backstairs.

Or maybe the murder was committed by somebody already in the house, one of the rest of us.

But why should Dulcy and Mr. Smith hate me enough to make the police think that I had killed two people, maybe three?

Burke said: "Inquest today. The coroner will ask you more questions, but I want to get back to work, Miss Jane. Inquest at two for Miss Lizzie, immediately afterward for Henry. Probably not until tomorrow for Madame Terracci, unless Doc gets a move on."

"What happens at an inquest?" I had some horrible notion that inquests had something to do with post mortem examinations, and I wondered fearfully if we would have to look on while the doctors made examinations of the bodies to see what the people had died of.

"Just questions, like these, only the coroner doesn't stop, the way I do, to have coffee. Make me a cup, maybe, Miss Jane?"

"Come downstairs in my own place and I'll make you as much as you please. And if you'll go down in the cellar with me to get it I'll give you strawberry jam with it, or quince jelly. If you'll send Curly down to the corner for a loaf of bread, I'll make toast. And if you want bacon and eggs, you'll have to buy them at the same time. But I can cook, and I haven't a vial of poison in the place, in spite of what Dulcy and Smith say, Mr. Burke."

Curly brightened up. "There's a butcher shop on the corner," he said. "Bacon and eggs would be swell, and I'll take a chance on the poison."

I gave him a long list of things I needed anyhow and some money from the extra cash my boss had given me, and laughed a little inwardly to consider that this was a funny way of painting the town red! Buying bacon and eggs and toast-bread for a couple of cops on a murder case.

Then Burke went along down into the cellar with me to get to the little bin where I kept my jams and jellies and preserves. The place must have been a wine cellar at one time. It was a little musty, but there's always soap and water in the house to wash off the outside of a jar. I gave Burke the key and listened to him gloat over the number of jars on the shelves. He speculated about what he might choose, if he stopped to read all the labels, and finally compromised on half a dozen small jars of various kinds. We found an old carton for carrying them upstairs in, and turned out the light and locked the door behind us. A flashlight would see us out of the cellar.

We were halfway up the stairs when I heard a click. I started to call Burke's attention to it when I realized that the mouse trap must have caught a victim. There were enough human victims in the house already, and I didn't want to have to look while Burke did something about the mouse, so I kept silent.

We washed up ourselves and the dusty jars and had the coffee made by the time that Curly came back with the bacon and eggs and toast-bread and the rest of my supplies. My toaster is the double kind, so I had a pile of slices ready when I slid the omelet out on the plate that held the crisp bacon, and drew up some chairs to the table. We were sitting down when I realized that Betty and Torry were supposed to be there in my room, and that I hadn't seen hide nor hair of them. Even the bed was freshly made, and there was no sign of the room having been disturbed at all.

I dropped the fork with which I had intended to spear some hot toast.

"Is Torry dead? Did he die here, in my room?" But Burke shook his head.

"He's in the hospital. They thought it would be better. He hasn't recovered consciousness. His wife is with him. He may recover, but it would be safer for him in the hospital."

"When did they take him away?" I hadn't heard anything.

"When you were upstairs instructing me about pancakes and strawberry jam. This omelet is good enough for any king, Miss Jane. Ever think of cooking for a living? You ought to make more than in an office."

"I'm thinking of setting up a tearoom some day."

"But you're not a reduced gentlewoman," put in a voice from the half-open door," and in walked Riley, all neatly dressed in tweeds, a clean shave and collar making him much more spruce than reporters usually are.

He didn't ask for an invitation, but just came on in and poured himself a cup of coffee, took another plate from the sidetable and waded in like the rest of us.

Burke said, when the bacon and omelet were gone and he was falling to on the toast and jam: "Any objections to marrying me, Miss Jane?"

"I saw her first," objected Riley.

"But I brought home the bacon," offered Curly, and we all laughed.

"If this were a musical comedy," said Riley, "we'd all be going down on our knees now to propose in chorus. Then she'd pick one of us and the others would leave the stage."

"But not without the quince jelly," Burke said. "If you could only detect as you can cook, Miss Jane, you'd be a good addition to the police force."

"If you could only detect the way you can eat, Mr. Burke, you'd be a good addition yourself," I retorted, and didn't realize that I was giving Burke a good slap in the face with my joking words.

Curly and Riley began to talk very fast and with their mouths very full, and Burke said nothing but just kept watching me, while I figured out that as a diplomat I made a good cook. How did I know that my silly words were going to make a tragedy out of what had started to be a sort of breakfast party?

But after all, it did seem that I had spent a huge proportion of my time fixing food for Burke and the rest. This was the third meal since early that morning, and, after all, a detective or a policeman is supposed to do something besides eat and ask questions of people who didn't do the murdering.

I couldn't even be certain that Burke considered me innocent, except that of course he wouldn't be likely to eat meals fixed for him by a girl who had the habit of poisoning. Guests at the Borgia board must have lost their taste for food along about the fourth murder.

Unless maybe he felt that if he ate enough meals with me and I was the murderer I'd try to poison him and then he'd have the evidence to convict me. It did seem like overemphasis on duty, however, to use this method through three meals, with probably more to come.

My two brothers and I had been alone in the world since I was twelve, except for my late grandfather and an aunt as vague and fluttery as a butterfly, and she had died last year. I was a lot more domestic than most eighteen-year-old girls, which accounted for the jams, and for a certain light hand I had with omelets, but I didn't have any of the "background" that the newspapers talked about the next day. I did seem to be all alone in a vacuum, some-how, because there wasn't anybody except my brothers I could go back home to. But I still think that there wasn't any reason at all for the newspapers to think that it was suspicious that I didn't have much family or many friends to rally around me. Of course they didn't come right out and say that it was suspicious, but a hint is as good as a wallop, and until Riley came down and found me crying over somebody's sob column, I didn't realize that anybody understood how I felt. But that was a couple of days later.

There were people coming and going for hours, it seemed to me, asking a thousand questions and being mys-terious about things that sounded perfectly simple to me. Riley did manage to sick a few reporters in other direc-tions by doing a little important telephoning and getting himself assigned to stick around and report other murders as they happened. That's the way he explained it, any-how, although it did sound a lot like play-by-play baseball broadcasts to me.

At any rate, I swept policemen and reporters from un-der my feet all day, until the hour of the inquest when we had to go along, the bunch of us, to the coroner's. There wasn't any sort of dignity about the room to which we went. I had mixed up the words for inquest and autopsy and had expected a sort of hospital laboratory, but my re-lief at seeing a table and a bunch of folding chairs couldn't take away my feeling that there should be something more dignified about the inquiry. Because death is a big thing, an important thing, and it should be handled with more seriousness than you'd pay to a business conference on the tuna fish industry, say. Yet the conference on the tuna fish industry had taken place the week before in my boss's mahogany and glass office, and when I compared the carpeted floors, the polished furniture and the paneled walls of the conference with the folding campchairs and the bare splintered floors of the inquest, death seemed like a much less important thing than the tuna fish industry.

That isn't really a part of my story. At any rate, we listened to the coroner, who turned out to be the man that Burke had called Doc. Only he wasn't the same man who had ministered to Torry in my room the night before.

And Burke turned out to be Detective Inspector Burke, and important enough to get respect for his opinions from everybody present.

They worked out the answers to a lot of things that seemed to puzzle them, but the results of the inquiry were simply murder by person or persons unknown.

The other two inquests didn't bring out a thing that was new, so there's no use going into detail about them. Still, there were a few points that I noted, and I want to put them down here just to get things straight. The list of us, for one thing:

Mrs. Meyer looked more beautiful than ever with a sort of mature loveliness. It was beauty of bone and movement and manner, chiefly. Her eyes were deepset and glowing, and when she answered questions I could see the lines faintly penciled around her eyes and mouth, which made her look older and haggard but somehow even more beautiful. She spoke in a low, throaty, toneless voice, like a singer who sings only in a minor key. She was very deaf, but the coroner didn't shout at her. That ageless beauty and the dignity of her manner gave him added consideration. She established the fact, after written questions

were handed to her, that she hadn't heard Broad come in,
that she hadn't been awake until Riley had sent Madame
Terracci down to awaken her in her basement apartment
after the second death was discovered. She hadn't seen
either body. She hadn't talked to any of the three victims
for over a week except Madame Terracci at the time she
had awakened her, and then "we said little. We were too
shocked for words. But I must tell you one thing. Henry's
ghost still walks. I saw Henry after his death. He walked
along the hall and I saw him in the doorway of the room
where we all sat. I saw him as clearly as I see you now," she
said very simply to the coroner. I put that down word for
word in my notes because the memory of it was clear to me
even hours after it happened.

Nobody else had seen Henry's ghost except Dulcy, and
she acted so important about it that the assembly was un-
believing. Dulcy looked like the kind of a girl who makes
things up so people will pay attention to her, so everybody
discounted half of what she said.

That turned out to be a mistake, but we didn't know it
then. Honest grief for the loss of a lover is one thing, and
Dulcy's dramatics were another.

As usual she dressed the part. Her dress was black with
crisp white bands at throat and wrist. Her hat had a black
veil thrown back from the face, framing her trite pretti-
ness with mourning. Her curls were carefully set, and only
a shade too brassy for belief. Her nails were too long and
too sharp. And she had changed their color to a sort of
second-mourning mauve. Her shoes were black, with some
sort of tricky platform arrangement instead of heels, her
toenails entirely visible through the sandal toes, and the
chiffon stockings were the same shade as her fingernails.

She went into hysterics, she cried, she moaned and she
fainted, during her various periods as a witness, but nothing new came out of her recitals except the announcement

that she had seen me come out of my door, go along the hall to the front stairway, go up the stairs toward Madame Terracci's room, and that I had a box of candy in my hand. She insisted on this and on the box of candy, just as she insisted that she had seen Henry's ghost. Since I knew that her evidence about me was a lie, I took it for granted that her other evidence was lying, too. And that set me off in the wrong direction, although it didn't fool Burke at all. It seems that he had known other women like Dulcy. She was new to me. Back home in Bridgeport, there hadn't been a Dulcy in the whole place, unless you count Marybelle Rafferty who played the star part in the high school play and who put on airs for a long time afterwards until her boy friend started going with that plain girl in the parsonage. After that Marybelle got back to normal soon enough.

Riley was a real comfort to me. He testified that he had seen Dulcy at the head of the stairs on the second floor and that I couldn't possibly have come upstairs without him seeing me, since he was watching Dulcy. The coroner asked him whether he could have seen me if I had come up the back stairs, and he insisted stoutly that he could. I wasn't any too sure of that myself, but of course I hadn't gone up any stairs at all, and I knew it, although nobody seemed likely to believe me.

Mr. Smith, for some reason, seemed entirely in cahoots with Dulcy. In fact, he agreed with her so much that Riley said to me later: "It sounds like Cahoots has a case of Dulcyitus too. Sort of: 'You lie and I'll stick to it.'"

"Cahoots?" Funny that he should use the word when I'd just thought about him being in cahoots with Dulcy. Riley had the same idea, too.

"That's what we guys call him there at the house. He's an expert on so many questions, so he says. He knows so much about money that he must be in cahoots with the millionaires. He knows so much about medicine and law, to hear him tell it, that he's certainly in cahoots with the doctors and lawyers. So we call him 'Cahoots.' And now he's in Cahoots with Dulcy."

This made Smith seem like a real person instead of just a sort of feeble understudy to Burke. I studied him carefully, but aside from a slight wiry figure, not more than five foot five, thin brown hair, vague colorless eyes, and a gray unobtrusive suit, there wasn't actually anything about him to remember.

It seemed strange to think of somebody I knew doing his best to get me arrested for murder, but Cahoots Smith went at the job as if it were his one ambition in life. You could see that his idea of a comfortable seat for me was the electric chair. It wasn't only his vindictive manner. It was the decisive way he said things, as if there were no doubt that the things were true. He saw me other places where I hadn't been. I had been seen in the lower hall starting to creep upstairs at about two o'clock on the night of the murders. It was entirely possible that I had been in the lower hall at that time or a little later because I hadn't seen a clock or watch when I'd opened the door to Broad. But certainly I hadn't been "creeping upstairs." And I thought that two-thirty would have been nearer the time.

Mrs. Meyer had reported seeing Torry in the house after eight, and more than one witness mentioned hearing Madame Terracci say that she had seen Torry going into Henry's room with a box of candy in his hand. But Madame Terracci wasn't there to speak for herself, and poor Torry was lying in a hospital still unconscious, although Betty was with us, looking tiny and fragile and terrified, and only half awake.

The Basque lad with the limp and the German boy with the scar on his face hadn't seen or heard anything, and so they were permitted to pack and move up to the third-floor room (in the same house) that they had picked out

last week. The other young chaps up there were out of the
running, too, so that just left the first and second floor
groups on the stage in the spotlight, as Riley put it. Except that somehow I kept feeling that with all of the rest
of the city around us, it was unreasonable for the police to
suspect only the people on two floors in one house.

Torry. Betty. Mrs. Meyer. Mr. Cahoots Smith. Dulcy.
Riley. Broad, who had started the whole business with his
ring at the door. If Bill Broad hadn't left his key in his other pants, then maybe I wouldn't have had any more connection with the whole business than the ash-blond girl
named Johnson who roomed with Dulcy and who hadn't
appeared except for a minute last night and now at the inquests. She didn't know anything, she didn't manufacture
any knowledge that she didn't really have, and certainly
she wasn't being suspected of any murder. She sat in the
chair as placid as a piece of blank paper while the fury of
the discussion went around her.

And then, suddenly, out of all the questions came one
insistent fact:

George was still gone.

He hadn't been seen in the house since before all of
these murders.

And it took all of Burke's ingenuity to persuade the coroner's jury not to bring in a verdict of murder by George.

But George was still gone. And whether he was murderer or murder victim we were not to know until much later.

9

Now that I read all of the detective novels, I see that they spend huge numbers of pages talking about the questions and answers at inquests, and about the things that the police do to establish the facts of the death. But then these things didn't seem quite so important to me. True, I sat through inquests on all three of the victims and later on still another murdered person. But facts were drowned in words, and I find that even now I keep remembering facts about the characters, the actors, instead of the things they said. Besides, I knew most of the answers they gave, and it's interesting to study faces and hands and to listen to the tones of voices instead of listening to actual words. People seldom manage to get the exact meaning of their thoughts into finished sentences, anyhow. I know I don't.

I keep remembering the way Mrs. Meyer carried her head and the utter quiet of her body, even her hands. Only her lips moved, when she answered the questions. The only time she was at all disturbed was when she talked about seeing Henry's ghost:

"I looked up," she said, "and the candles flickered and there he stood. I could see his face faintly, in the half-light. It was Henry—nobody else. I don't know whether he was looking at me. I don't remember his eyes. They seemed far away, as if they weren't alive. And his face looked dead, too, and stiff, like a mask of death." I was to remember that "mask of death" again later, but then I just kept wondering why Mrs. Meyer should have been so disturbed when she talked about Henry's death and not even ruffled at the details about Miss Lizzie and Madame Terracci.

Dulcy was as vindictive a little brat as I ever saw. You could just see her going after every man in the place and getting most of them. Not Riley. Somehow I thought he could see through her, but maybe that was just because it made me mad to think that she could pull the wool over every man's eyes just because she was pretty and oozed sex. She was so obvious, but maybe men like their women labelled, so they can see, from the beginning, what they are. I've always thought that it must be a woman who manufactured that gag about woman's mystery attracting men.

Bill Broad was unexpectedly handsome. I hadn't noticed him much before the night I opened the door for him just before he discovered the first murder. But his business suit was as well tailored as the dinner clothes he had worn that night, and his shirt collars fit him. Most men's collars don't. His hands were nice, too, the hands of an artist, and I don't mean the slim effeminate hands that most people call artistic. Most real artists have strong hands, sure of motion, powerful of gesture. Broad's hands were like that. I knew a sculptor once with such hands and a pianist who should have stayed on the concert stage and not let himself get sidetracked into teaching. There was a painter, too, who managed, with hands like that, to do an amazing job with oils.

Broad's hands were much more interesting than anything he had to say on any of these three occasions. He just repeated the things he had already said. He even reported that he had forgotten to call the police after getting the operator the first time and had to go back later, and I felt like a fool when I realized that I had suspected him of deliberately delaying the call to the police.

Riley blandly denied cutting the telephone wire, although he could make no explanation of the reason why he had been messing around it when Mr. Smith had seen him. I had seen him, too, but I made no mention of that fact. There were several other things I didn't mention. If all persons in a murder case keep as many things to themselves as Riley and I did, then it's a wonder to me that any murder case is ever "cracked," as Riley called it.

There are still a few other things that I noticed during those sessions. I had expected to be accused of something in connection with the discovery of Torry on the balcony outside my window, as well as the bloodspot on my robe, the blood on the coins, and the splash of blood on the mantelpiece. But there was only a perfunctory mention of these, and when I said that I knew nothing about them, nobody pressed the questions.

Nobody seemed to think it suspicious that Torry should have been outside my window on my balcony without me knowing anything about it, and to me that sounded like the most suspicious thing of all. Because, after all, it wasn't natural for them to believe me when I said that I had slept through everything, that so far as I knew nobody had come into my room since my early bedtime.

They tried to get me to say that somebody might have come in while I was at the door, but that wasn't likely. And although it would have been an easy way out for me, it just wasn't possible for anybody to drag a half-dead man through a room in the dark and dump him on a balcony without making any noise, and that's what must have happened if their idea had been valid.

It's true that I had had my bathrobe on inside out that first time, and I mentioned that when we were trying to find out when the bloodstain had come on the pocket, but we didn't get any further than that.

The ash-blond girl named Johnson didn't seem any more vivid when she was testifying than she did at any other time. I kept wondering, all through those three sessions, what in the world had drawn her and Dulcy together. They had roomed together for years, so the girl said. None of Dulcy's artificial color had come off on the Johnson girl, and somehow it seemed important to me that it never had. After all, girls who room together for years sometimes use each other's make-up and clothes, but these never did. The Johnson girl didn't know anybody any better than she knew me, and that was not at all. But she did say one thing that I kept thinking of afterwards, and that was:

"Henry loved Dulcy enough to kill Miss Lizzie if Miss Lizzie separated them. And how do you know that Henry didn't kill Madame Terracci too? Maybe he put a poisoned chocolate with regular ones so she got it after he died. Maybe Henry murdered Madame Terracci and Miss Lizzie too."

That was just a little too easy to be believed. The police raised their eyebrows at the ease of it, because, as Burke said, even the easy jobs aren't that obvious.

The Basque boy and the German appeared, had nothing to say and went their way out of our lives. Probably Mrs. Meyer and Dulcy saw them later, but I didn't except for those three sessions. The same with those other three men on the top floor. That left Riley, Broad, Mrs. Meyer, Dulcy, the Johnson girl, Cahoots Smith, Betty and Torry, and me. Oh, I almost forgot the mailman. He was a funny tall man, as thin as a spider, rather hunched at one shoulder from carrying a mailbag for many years. He had studied to be a minister, he told me once, and had then concluded that he wasn't good enough, so he chose another method of bringing news to the world. He was up and out at some ungodly hour and none of us saw him much. The only time in weeks that I had seen him was in the hall at the time of the first murders and in the room where we were all gathered after the light went out.

He had a clean slate, from the beginning, I think. The only reason I mention him at all here was because of something rather odd that happened at the time of the next murder, and his final big scene in which he played the star role.

I slept in my own room the next night and there were no interruptions to sleep. We knew that there was a policeman somewhere in the house, and Burke advised me, aside, that he'd picked one who'd be impervious to Dulcy. He didn't say it that way, but it's what he meant.

I tumbled into bed with a callous disregard for everything except my desire for sleep, and when I woke up the sun was peering in at the window and there were no new bloodstains.

I opened wide the balcony window, as soon as I had dressed, and stood there looking out at the place where Torry had been. There was no trace of blood or disorder.

The rubber plant that I had bought as the only indestructible plant for cities was as dusty and tired as if there had been no rain. Somehow, looking at that silly plant made me wonder why I had ever thought it would be fun to live in a big city where, as the old actor said: "The streetcars go boom", only instead of streetcars it is usually subways and automobiles and trucks.

I had had coffee and was buttering a piece of toast when Riley's knock came at the door.

He came in and waited to be offered some breakfast before he sat down. That was more than Burke did, later, when he came in. He knew where I kept the cups, and he filled his and looked around for the cream before he said a word. Riley hadn't started to talk, either, so we had a silence filled with the glub of cream coming out of a can and the crunching of toast.

"No further casualties this morning, I gather," Riley said finally.

"Read the *Standard* and find out," Burke said. "Listen, kid, you could make a mass murder mystery out of swatting flies. Don't you think that you've rather overdone the praying death and poisoned chocolate headlines today?"

"It's my job," Riley reminded him, "when I'm not bumming breakfast from Jane." He grinned at me.

Burke finished his third cup of coffee and his fourth piece of toast with jam. He carefully wiped his buttery fingers on my best damask napkin and took an envelope out of his pocket.

"There, Riley," he said, "does this look like a clue? Know what it is? Don't answer, Miss Jane. I want Riley's answer."

The crisp brown scrap in his hand was like a bit of starched brown paper cut in a lace pattern, as if somebody had scorched one of those lace doilies that some bakeries use for displays under cream puffs.

It took a minute before I realized what it was, and I knew that Riley hadn't a notion whether it was fish, fowl or good red herring.

At least he looked bewildered. Burke wouldn't let him touch it, and Riley said finally:

"I don't know whether it's animal, vegetable or mineral. Am I supposed to guess? What score did the others make on this Information Quiz program?"

"This is my job. Can't you guess, Riley?"

"Well, it might be a piece torn from somebody's lace dress. Is it? Madame Terracci had something like that once. Remember, Jane? With the yellow rose on the shoulder? She wore it when she sang at your birthday party last month."

"It's a good guess," Burke said, writing something down in his little notebook, after he put the brown thing back in its envelope.

"I notice that you didn't ask me," I said, ready to show off. Because of course I knew. It was right in my line.

"Your chance comes later, Miss Jane. I'm on my way to get another answer, first. Want to come along? I may need a witness. You may be needed, besides, to tell me whether it's exactly the right answer."

I put away the food and left the cups and saucers for Riley's reluctant services, after pointing out the dishtowels, soap and dishpan. It must be nice to have somebody to help with the dishes. Besides, if I could cook for people, they ought to help with the dishes, I thought.

We went next to Mrs. Meyer's basement apartment. The house was one of those old places built on a hillside street. The basement apartment was on the level of a garden at the back of the house, and the sunshine was streaming in at the east window where a canary in his cage was singing.

I've never been much for caged birds, myself. I don't like the idea of bars for birds any more than my small-town training permits me to like them in most houses, but the cheerfulness of this bird spoke well for his spirits, and the woman who turned to greet us probably needed cheerfulness.

Mr. Burke wrote something on a pad that he took out of his pocket and passed it to Mrs. Meyer. She answered in her soft monotone, a little more throaty than the voice of most deaf people:

"No. I can't hear the bird very well, but I know that he's singing, and he's company for me. I keep goldfish, too. Canaries and goldfish are the only two pets you can keep in a place like this without disturbing your tenants. I like pets. I had a cat once that was almost like a child. She was so smart she almost talked. Why, that cat knew more than most people, I always said."

I could tell from the way she went on talking without saying anything that she was nervous. But no fumbling of hands nor turn of head betrayed her. She was as beautiful as ever, as serene of manner as a statue carved of ice.

Burke wrote something else when we had taken the seats she offered us. He handed her the pad, and she nodded when she had read his words.

"I've said everything I know," she said. "I didn't hear anything. I did see Mr. Torrence in the house early in the evening, but I didn't see him later. And I can't help it if I feel that you, Miss Jane, know some more about Madame Terracci, besides what you've told. Because else why should she leave you all that money when you've got a job and don't need it?"

The resentment in her voice was strong. I'd almost forgotten about the money, that morning, although I hadn't had much chance to forget about it the day before. Every two minutes during the inquest on Madame Terracci somebody had said something about the legacy, and I couldn't understand the resentment, any more than I could understand why she had left things to me in the first place. Certainly nobody, including me, had ever considered that she had any money. As a matter of fact, one of the reasons why I'd so often taken coffee to her, or rolls or cake when I baked, or jam or jelly, was that I couldn't feel that she had enough to eat with her pathetic factory salary after her long luxurious years.

The last thing in the world that I expected was a legacy from her. She was poor, I'd thought, and I'd do what I could to help. And now to have everybody in the house resenting that was too much. But had they known about the legacy at all, when they began to show their dislike?

I'd never been one, even at eighteen, to waste much time pondering about whether people liked me. If they did, well and good, and if they didn't, then they didn't need to stick around. But this was different. Because, after all, I'd dug in there, and had planned to stay for a while, and it's not too pleasant to live in the same house with people who hate you.

Burke kept on writing his little notes on the pads and tucking them into his pocket after she'd answered the questions. She didn't answer any new questions for a long time, and then, casually, Burke took out of his pocket the envelope containing the crisp brown scrap that Riley had thought was part of a brown dress that Madame Terracci once had. The dress was taffeta and this scrap wasn't anything like taffeta, but that didn't matter then.

I watched Mrs. Meyer's face when Burke took out the brown thing and held it on his palm. She was always pale, but she turned a little paler, I thought, although she said nothing. I certainly couldn't tell, from anything she said or did, whether or not she could identify the thing. After a few more perfunctory questions and answers, we got up and left and went on upstairs again, heading for Bill Broad's room.

I stopped when Burke had his hand raised to knock on the door. "Listen, Mr. Burke," I said, "do you want to know what that is? Because I can tell you. It's the edge of a pancake, the thin lacy edge of a pancake that's baked exactly the way that Madame Terracci baked them. Did you know that?"

"I suspected it. How did you know? So far nobody else has known. This might be anything. Riley thought it was part of a dress. Mrs. Meyer didn't know what it was and refused to guess. By the way, that woman hates you. You'd better get out of this place as soon as you can after the case is over. A nasty landlady can ruin a girl's reputation in this man's town, you know."

"This is ridiculous. Why should I get out of a one-room apartment that I've fixed up exactly the way I want it because of a landlady who is beautiful but venomous? You make her sound like the wicked stepmother in *Snow White*."

"And isn't she? Has it occurred to you that Mrs. Meyer may have known what this brown thing was, that she has known everything about all of these murders, and that—" He stopped and became casual again.

I finished his sentence for him in a doubtless annoying way I had. I almost whispered: "Mrs. Meyer may be the murderer herself. No."

But in a way I hoped that the guess was right. Horrible as it would be to think of Mrs. Meyer as the murder, yet it was easier than to think of Torry, or Riley, or Betty or Bill Broad, and they, I had to acknowledge, were the realest possibilities, especially Torry.

Burke raised his hand and knocked on the door. Once. Twice.

And it sounded like the knock of doom.

But there was no answer from behind the panel of the heavy door.

Was there death behind that door too?

10

Burke turned the knob of the door behind which silence dwelt.

How silly of me to be upset! But I kept remembering the night when Bill Broad had stood outside a door and had come in to find murder. Now we were outside and he was inside. And had murder come again?

The door opened. Inside, everything was quiet except for the ticking of a clock. With sudden shock I realized that we had come into the room where last I had seen Henry's body lying on a bed in its last sleep. Now Henry was gone, and on the other bed lay a figure, fully clad.

Burke was there, touching him, looking at him, before I could urge my feet toward him at all. But I knew who it was. Bill Broad this time—murdered—and beside him some more chocolates. The house was a hotbed of them. After this I'd never want to taste chocolates, and it took me months to be able to look a chocolate layer cake in the face.

But as we watched, I thought that I saw Bill Broad move one of his strong hands. I whispered: "He's alive. He's breathing."

"NO! Yes, he is, too!" And Burke had his hands on Bill Broad, sniffing at his lips, acting utterly unlike his usual casual self.

"Get out of here, Miss Jane. Get downstairs. Call this number." He penciled a number on his pad and handed it to me. "Tell Doc to get here as quickly as possible. Say the case is exactly like Madame Terracci's, so far as I can tell, but the man isn't dead—yet. Speed it up, Miss Jane. I'll do what I can in the meantime." He was between me and Bill Broad, so I couldn't see what he did when he bent over the figure on the bed, and I got out of there more quickly than I'd gone when Henry had been there, even.

I delivered the message and then hesitated about whether I'd better go back up and help. But Riley would know—and Riley was washing up after breakfast. No. That had been almost an hour ago. He'd be back upstairs where he belonged, or else he'd be gone to work. He did have a job, and there must be other assignments in town besides this one for him.

I opened my door, and there, sitting in my big chair, was Riley. He was tight asleep. Or was it sleep? Frightened, I came closer and bent down to see.

His voice was gentle. "Try the left cheek first," he said with his eyes still closed. "It's nearer the heart, they say, and responds better to kisses."

"You're crazy. I wasn't going to kiss you. I was just looking to see if you were dead."

"Then you were doing it pretty calmly, I'll say, Jane. Would you be sorry?"

"Probably not. But you're not the victim—this time."

He sat up quickly: "Was there another?"

"Yes. Bill Broad."

"Good Lord. There goes my case." I didn't know then what he was talking about, but he showed me later the brilliant piece of work, action imagined and entirely unsupported by evidence. He had Bill all worked out as the murderer, of course without evidence or any grain of proof that Bill had any reason for wanting to kill any one of the three, let alone injuring Torry. But that was his case. And it was dead on its feet. There wasn't any case. Because Bill Broad was a victim, although a still breathing victim. And maybe he could tell Burke who had poisoned him.

I told Riley what little I knew, and it was little enough.

"Stay here," he said. He telephoned his office, and I heard him give a few pithy sentences. Then he rang off and loped upstairs three steps at a time and went into Bill Broad's room without knocking. He closed the door behind him, and I sat down.

So here we were, back where we started from, with Bill Broad in the spotlight. This time I felt more than a slight feeling of loss at the idea of his death. It was partly, I guess, because he was so young and handsome. No eighteen-year-old girl ever hears of the death of an attractive young man without wondering what might have been his fate if he had lived. This was more than that. Broad and Riley and I had been a sort of team in the beginning before Burke came along to take Broad's place. True, Riley had distrusted Broad, but without any real knowledge or evidence. And now there were so few of us left. The murderer might strike anywhere. Worse than that was the terror that comes from not knowing why murder is striking. The motive of murder is as important as the method or the opportunity, probably more important.

And so long as we didn't know why the mass murderer was striking at the inhabitants of these light housekeeping apartments, there was always the faint fear that just living there was dangerous, that the murderer might have it in his mind to eradicate everybody in the house for some reason of his own.

It sounds so simple to say it now, after all this time, but then I sat, in all the misery of my eighteen years, shaking with terror, trying to keep what little serenity was left.

There wasn't any work to do—Riley had done it all, bless him. So I just sat, wondering what was going to happen.

And at that minute, three things happened.

Hordes of men came in at the street door. One was certainly the doctor. With him were a couple of others who were probably members of the homicide squad I hadn't seen yet.

One was a telegraph boy who stopped to ask directions from the doctor and who then came straight to me and held out a telegram and his book for me to sign.

The rest were reporters. From time to time I had thought that it might be fun to be a reporter. You meet so many interesting people, they all say. Well, if this was being a reporter, then I wanted none of it. Riley belonged there, so I didn't much mind him prying around and asking questions. But this gang—they were ghouls. The women were worse than the men, I thought. One of them had bright red hair and a jacket suit that almost matched it. Maybe she had dyed the hair to match the suit. I once knew a girl who bought an automobile to match a favorite hat. She was the first rich girl I'd ever known. That was the year that she ran away with her chauffeur and got disinherited by her parents.

One girl called: "Let's see the heiress. Was it a million the way they say?"

A tall man with a camera in one hand and in the other a sort of electric light bulb with crumpled silvery paper in it flashed a light on me, and he and several other people snapped some pictures of me standing there frowning and trying to make out whether the same man was holding the camera and making the light or whether it was two different men.

I couldn't see with the light in my eyes, and I was too bewildered to understand.

I didn't have time to open the telegram. I didn't even realize I was still holding it till the redheaded girl called: "Read us your news. It looks like more excitement."

Then the rescue came. The homicide squad men and the doctor had gone upstairs, and at the moment when I was just about ready to cut and run myself, even if it was toward murder, just so long as it was away from this gang, Riley came. He stood there at the head of the stairs, looking down, and if the grin on his face wasn't beatific then I hope never to see an angel.

"Hi-yah, gang!" he said with a casual flutter of the hand. The casual tone was worthy of Burke.

First they didn't notice him at all, and then they all hailed him indignantly. "News, boys and gals," he said in a stage whisper. "But come outside. There's a tea-house up the street. Join me in a cup of tea."

"If it's big enough for all of us," added the redheaded girl, laughing as if she thought that her gag was new and original. "And must it be tea?"

"Tomorrow's pay day," explained Riley, "and tea is cheaper than beer. Now if anybody offered to finance a stein of beer I might be persuaded."

Like some Pied Piper, he led them all out and poked his head around the door before he closed it. His grin was worth money.

And I got myself together and got back in my room, with my door locked behind me, before I stopped trembling.

I wasn't a trembling wildflower, even at eighteen, but it had been a strange experience, being thrown to the lions that way. I had my first real experience of mass psychology that day. Every one of those reporters was probably a grand person, good company and good to his maiden aunt. But put them all together and they added up to something just a little wilder than the wolves they toss babies to in the old Russian melodramas.

My telegram was from my boss. He must have had a few drinks in Chi at the convention, and the headlines about the murders at our house must have reminded him of his last words about painting the town red. The telegram read:

"When I said what I did on Thursday, or was it Wednesday or Friday, I didn't mean for you to murder the whole household. Couldn't you content yourself with one or two?"

It was the boss' idea of humor. I didn't doubt it. I hadn't been able to talk him out of sending a telegram of congratulation to a friend who had lost an adored mother-in-law. The boss would be like that. I could only thank my lucky stars that the telegram had come directly to me instead of falling into the hands of the police. Innocent that I was then, I didn't realize that it would be an easy job for Burke to get the text of any telegram that sounded suspicious.

I tore the yellow paper into neat strips and burned them carefully in an old iron cooking pot I'd picked up in an antique shop. I opened the window to let the smoke smell out, and smoked two quick cigarettes in succession so I'd have some more familiar-looking ashes to cover the paper ashes that I put in my big ashtray.

I was very thorough, too thorough. It took me a long time, and by the finish of the period I was so nervous that I jumped when Riley's knock came at the door.

He looked tired when I let him in. He was relaxed, though, and had obviously had a couple of glasses of beer—not enough to make him drunk,

just enough to make his tongue a little less bridled than usual.

I thanked him for getting rid of the reporters, and he held out his hand and said: "Gimme."

I wasn't quite sure whether he wanted to shake hands or to grab a cup of coffee, but he added: "The telegram.

Haven't I earned the right to read it? Burke won't show me, but I want to know. How can I keep up with you if I don't see the telegram?"

"But—I—no, it's personal, and I don't see why I should show it to you."

"Come. Come. Papa spank. Even if it's the best boyfriend, it won't hurt you to say so. Gimme, girl."

"But—" my gaze wandered involuntarily to the ashtray—"I haven't got it any more. It's gone. It was just from my boss, who's in Chicago. Business instructions," I lied blandly.

"Yes? Sounds like it. Then why did Burke look so upset when he got the wire over the phone? I heard him ask Western Union to report to police headquarters the wire just sent to you, and then he phoned his office, and when he heard what they said, his face was as long as a baseball game to a chess player."

"It was a joke," I told him truthfully but feebly, and he just stood there, shaking his head at me, when Burke's knock came on the door.

His voice was casual, and he sat down in the big chair as if he'd just dropped in at the kitchen door to have a word of cheer with the cook.

"Get out, Riley," he said. "You've made enough headlines today. I want to talk to Jane."

"But I sicked the rest of the reporters on a guy across the river, so they would let us alone," he said. "Listen, Burke. I gave 'em a perfectly good scoop on the Thompson case just in order to get 'em to let me alone here to take care of Jane—and you," he added blandly.

"You're too late with the Thompson case. The guy's dead. Kinders, you mean?"

"Dead! When?"

"This morning. His housekeeper killed him and confessed to the other murders too—Thompson and Mrs.

Thompson. She's in the cooler now. Your police reporter is on the story, probably."

Riley looked as disappointed as a kid whose ice-cream cone has dropped in the mud. "Well—" he began feebly, and Burke used only a few more well-put words to shove him out and to turn to me.

"I had you in the clear, Jane. You were a good girl because you made coffee for me and liked old Terracci. I'm as dense as a cub reporter with a new assignment. Why did you let me make a fool of myself? You look like a good kid. Would you want somebody else to go to the chair for your crimes?"

Such decisive words and such a casual tone. And for the life of me I couldn't tell whether he really thought that I was guilty or not. And Riley was off to nowhere again, so I couldn't look to him.

"But I—I didn't. Honestly I didn't, Mr. Burke."

Burke permitted himself the ghost of a grin. "No? Then explain the wire."

"It's just my boss' idea of a joke. He is like that after three drinks. I remember one time—" And I went off into an involved story about the time that the boss decided it would be fun to pretend that his house was haunted when his spiritualist maiden aunt visited him. I was pretty vague, I'm afraid, and got lost in my own words, chiefly because of my fright and the incredulous expression on Burke's face, but I came to the end of it eventually.

"I've put the office in touch with this. They're contacting your boss at the other end. We'll get the story straight. Maybe I shouldn't have let you tag along with me. It just gave you a better opportunity to commit all the rest of the murders. Who're you picking next?"

"But you don't really believe that? Haven't you got a lie detector or something in your pocket so you can tell that I mean what I say?" His grin was more than casual that time, but he said nothing about my assumption that the lie detector was something like a cigarette case to be carried around in your pocket. Later I became acquainted with the blood pressure equipment that makes up the so-called lie detector and blushed for my sins.

Now I think that the amusement Burke got out of the mistake was worth the trouble he went to in putting on his act. Because the telegram was obviously as transparent to him as it was to me. He wasn't in doubt about the burning of it, either. He sniffed for a minute, then followed his nose straight to the ashtray, edged aside the cigarette stubs and ashes with the point of a pencil and said:

"People read fiction and they get the idea that if they put things in perfectly obvious places nobody'll look for 'em. Just for the record, I could find out what the paper was and make a pretty fair attempt at reconstruction even if you burned it. Most people don't know that. Next time scatter the ashes or put 'em down the drain if you want to hide something from me. But you won't. Old Eagle-Eye Burke can read your telegram out of the air."

He held an imaginary paper in front of his eyes and declaimed, but not very dramatically:

"For the next murder follow my directions and don't deviate, or you will pay the price yourself."

With eyes as big as billiard balls I listened, not knowing in my literal mind whether this telegram was as imaginary as his announcement of reading it from the air.

For the telegram that he recited was not the telegram that had been delivered to me, and that I had burned.

"Mr. Burke," I said sharply, "stop fooling and tell me really—was that the wire that was supposed to have been sent me?"

"Of course," he said. "I got the office to get me a copy after I saw the boy deliver yours. Wasn't that what you just burned?"

"My telegram said: 'When I said what I did on Thursday, or was it Wednesday or Friday, I didn't mean for you to murder the whole household. Couldn't you content yourself with one or two?' That's my boss' idea of humor. That was the wire I burned."

Burke was more excited than I'd ever seen him. "You're telling the truth?"

"I've been telling the truth straight along and nobody has believed me," I wailed.

"Then for the next three hours until I can get back here you sit tight in your own room, with door and windows locked. Don't move out of the place, not even for food. Because you are definitely in danger. I'll post a guard outside, and you stay here!"

As he had his hand on the door another knock came, and it was a policeman in uniform with a yellow envelope in his hand. "A Western Union boy left this a few minutes ago for Miss Jane," he said, and Burke handed me the wire.

"For the next murder follow my directions and don't deviate or you will pay the price yourself," it said. The wire was unsigned. I handed it to Burke.

Then, as the door slammed behind him, I locked it and sank down on my bed, ready for rest.

11

For three hours nothing was to happen, I thought. Not a thing. It seems incredible to talk of being thoroughly bored in the middle of a murder case, but I was. For one thing, I'm not used to solitary leisure. Of course I might have washed windows or scrubbed the floor or something like that, but even boredom can't drive me into being a good housekeeper. I might have taken a nap, but now that I had the opportunity I wasn't a bit sleepy. I was afraid, but not afraid enough to be panicky and nervous. Strange that I wasn't more afraid that murder might be turned on me now that it had come to stay in our house. But you never think that things like that can happen to you, even if they happen in the same house. Or maybe I was just less emotional than most girls of eighteen. After all this time, I find that I don't remember my own fright half so much as I remember the things that other people did, and said.

There were apples on my grocery list, so I made some apple-sauce and then, out of a clear sky, decided to make gingerbread to go with it. Luckily the stuff was now all in the house, and I slapped my ingredients down on the table and got into a clean white apron and washed up with all the fervor of a surgeon preparing for a major operation.

It was almost as easy to make a lot of it as a little, and it would save the trouble of making toast the next time Burke and Riley came around for a food handout.

That's the last time I ever baked gingerbread, incidentally. By this time I wouldn't know whether you use white sugar or brown or molasses, and whether you roll it out on a board or beat it in a bowl, and I don't want to know.

And if I hadn't decided to vary my flavoring a little, just to be different, I'd probably still be baking gingerbread every couple of weeks.

But it was three hours and a half later that trouble came from the gingerbread.

Soon its fragrance began to seep through the room and I felt more comfortable because of the heat from my little oven. But I was very lonesome and very curious about what was going to happen. The curiosity was worse than anything. Because I just can't sit down and do nothing. I'm not one of those who makes fancy work or plays bridge to pass the time, not when there are so many interesting people to talk to in the world, and it's better than going to the movies to listen to them.

These thoughts were passing through my mind when I thought suddenly of Bill Broad and something of the same kind he had said to me that night when he stood on the doorstep.

He had talked about wandering around after the theatre and talking to some derelicts who were on a park bench. I couldn't remember the exact words, but that was the idea. That wasn't the kind of talking I meant. That was a little too much like exploiting people who couldn't help themselves in order to pull out a sob story in return for a dime.

But if Broad had been to the theatre and had been walking around for hours afterwards, why hadn't he had a coat and hat with him? His sleeve was a little wet. I remembered that—just as if he had stood outside on the steps for a minute or two, but not enough wet for him to have gone walking after the theatre in the rising storm. Besides, the weather was chilly. He had an overcoat and a hat, nice ones. All of his clothes were nice. Then why hadn't he worn them to the theatre on a chilly night? And certainly if he had neglected wearing them, he would have come straight home to get them, before a long stroll in the storm.

Had Broad been somewhere else that night—somewhere close to home?

Had Broad seen something he should not have seen? And had the "something" caused his murder?

The gingerbread didn't burn because I was so preoccupied, but it just escaped it. I've always had to be single-minded in my cooking if I didn't want it to burn.

I didn't have an idea about who had sent me the second wire. That didn't sound like my boss at all. Peculiar as his sense of humor was, there wasn't anything vindictive about it, and there was about this wire.

Riley was on his way to get a story. Broad was either dead or dying. Mrs. Meyer was somewhere down in her basement apartment. Betty and Torry were at the hospital with Torry.

And I was slated to be the next victim, with some enemy planning to have me accused of the murder in case I escaped being killed myself.

Very pretty, but not so pretty as the gingerbread that I turned out of the pans a few minutes later. It stood on its wire cooling rack and looked so tempting that I longed to see somebody eating it.

I played with the idea of hailing the policeman outside or of asking him to take a piece down to Mrs. Meyer, but that would never do. And just as I was wondering, along came another knock at the door.

"Who is it?"

Dulcy's voice came from beyond the panel: "I want to talk to you, Jane. Let us in. Kay Johnson's with me."

Burke had told me to stay there, but he hadn't said anything about not having company. I didn't like Dulcy much,

but there were nine hundred and ninety-nine chances out
of a thousand that she hadn't had anything to do with the
murders, and certainly the Johnson girl was too colorless
ever to be a murderer, so I unlocked the door and locked
it again behind the girls. There was no sign in the hall of
the guard that Burke had mentioned. Maybe he'd stepped
out for a minute.

"You must be awful domestic," Dulcy said conversa-
tionally, in a party voice, settling herself in the rocking
chair like a little girl told by her mother to be on her good
behavior.

"I'm not. Isn't it funny," I remarked with equally inane
politeness, "how girls hate being told that they're domestic or even wholesome?"

"Maybe because they think that the gentlemen like girls
who ain't so domestic," offered Dulcy, self-consciously
bridling a little and settling a burnished wave of her hair.

I could just see her being superior. She was the charm-
ing blonde that gentlemen preferred, and I was the domestic kind who sat at home and darned stockings and made
cake. Of course I wasn't, really, having had my share of
boy-friends in my day.

But Dulcy had come for some definite reason, I was sure.
Now it was up to me to cut through all this mess of polite
wordiness and get the reason for which she had come.

The simplest way was to ask her: "Any special reason
for the visit, Dulcy?"

"No." She looked embarrassed. "Yes, there was, too.
Listen, Jane, what are you planning to do with all your
money after this business is over? How about you and me
going in business together?"

"But, Dulcy—" I couldn't help the dig—"I thought
that you thought I'd be well on my way to the electric
chair by the time that all this was over. Didn't you tell
Mr. Burke that you were sure that I poisoned the bunch

of them? And didn't you testify that I went upstairs when you know as well as I do that I didn't take one single step up that stairs? I was in the bathtub all the time, and if you had been listening instead of pulling that young cop away from his work you could have heard me splashing."

"Ain't he divine? Ain't he got the curliest hair you ever saw?" Dulcy's voice was tender, and I understood that love's young dream had again come to her.

It was Curly she was talking about, the young cop who had been talking to her instead of watching the stairways and the door to my room. And if I knew my Dulcy, and I thought I did, she had sent him or another cop away from the door now so she could come in.

I suspected that after telling lies about me she had suddenly come to realize that I was going to have some money and she wanted a share of it.

"What business?" I asked blandly, wondering what there was about this girl that got all the men. She couldn't talk, she hadn't any brains, her beauty wasn't real and natural the way that Mrs. Meyer's was. But she did get the men, somehow.

"The beauty business. I want to start a beauty shop. I've studied three methods and had special instruction in personality permanents besides. Will you, Jane? I got it all figured out. It wouldn't cost so much, and we'd get our money back in less than no time. How about it?"

Why—the girl really meant it. She wanted this more than I'd ever known her to want anything—even a man.

Something told me that it might be wiser to be on terms of armed neutrality or at least of a moderate friendliness toward Dulcy during the next few days, so I answered: "I haven't had a chance to figure out anything, and besides, they aren't sure of that will she left. If I get the money, I'll think about the idea very seriously and we'll talk about it later, Dulcy."

That had to satisfy her. So far the Johnson girl hadn't said a word. Now she murmured: "Let's go, Dulcy. I'm a little tired. I ate too much fish at lunch, I think."

"You need some bicarbonate of soda, I guess. Here— this soda'll do. Mind if I borrow the box on the shelf here, Jane?"

I couldn't say no, because she was walking toward my open supply cabinet and fingering the contents as she spoke. She took the box of baking soda and said: "This'll do. I'll bring it back this afternoon."

I locked the door after them, and still there was time to spare. I started to put away things, and then remembered the gingerbread. I hadn't been very hospitable not to offer some to the girls, so I opened the door again and called:

"Wait a minute, Dulcy, here's some gingerbread I baked." She came back halfway down the flight of stairs, and I reached up as high as I could to hand her a big chunk of gingerbread I'd cut and put on a plate.

Then I went back in and shut the door. I mention these things in detail because they became important afterwards, although at the time they seemed so trivial.

I cleared up then, and it took me a while to do that. I had almost finished the job when I heard a sharp ping outside my window and looked out, but

I couldn't see anything. It was probably a boy playing with a slingshot, I thought, and then went back to my job.

I must have been a little nervous, although I'm not, usually. At any rate, it was sheer carelessness that made me spill a whole bottle of vinegar on the table. I swore eighteen-year-old oaths when I saw that the other half of the loaf that I had given Dulcy was absolutely ruined by the vinegar, certainly unfit to eat. The garbage can got it and not the cake box, but that didn't really matter, because I had the other loaf, made with the other flavoring.

I have gone over and over these unimportant details trying to figure out if I've omitted anything, but I don't think I have. There were two loaves of gingerbread. One was made with the regular gingerbread mixture to which I'd added just a trace of vanilla. The other was the exact same mixture to which I'd added just a trace of the almond flavoring that was left over from some pudding I had made the week before. I told this over and over again, to Burke, to the coroner, to the rest of the police.

The bottle of almond extract had been bought at the corner grocery. It was exactly, so far as I knew, the same extract that I'd used for the pudding last week. And I had not thrown out the cake because I knew it was poisoned but because I had spilled vinegar on it, a whole bottle, so it was unfit to eat.

No matter how often I made these answers later, nobody believed me, and I want to put them down here, just as I remember them.

When I went to put away the vanilla I looked to see if I'd put away the almond, too, and it was nowhere to be seen. But I didn't look thoroughly. It might have been behind the flour can or the sugar, or a few jars of peaches and jam I'd just brought up from the cellar, or even behind the apple-sauce I'd just made. I didn't look thoroughly. So of course I couldn't swear, later, when they asked me whether I was certain that the flavoring was missing after I had talked to Dulcy.

The room was tidy, finally, and I pulled out a new magazine with a grand new serial. I cut a piece of the gingerbread, although it was a little too fresh to cut, really, and took a dish of the fresh apple-sauce and sat myself down with a tray of lunch or supper and the magazine.

It might have been almost any time. I'd forgotten to wind my watch and there wasn't a clock in the room. Like

most people who have to submit to routine, although they
hate it, I do without watches and clocks whenever I escape
the routine for a little. It makes me feel good to be able to
thumb my nose at a clock.

I sat there for a while eating gingerbread and enjoying
it thoroughly. The taste of vanilla was a little strange, but
I liked it because it seemed to tone up the molasses a little. I hadn't tasted the other loaf with the almond flavor,
but I made a mental note to try it again soon so I could
know whether the added flavors were really better than
plain gingerbread . . .

I haven't the least idea whether it was three hours or
four before Burke came back.

He looked tired, almost haggard, and I put the coffee
on again as soon as I saw him. "Look, I'm eating gingerbread," I told him. "I've just had some, and you can have
some too."

He slumped into the big chair and didn't say anything
for a while, and then he said: "Will gingerbread help when
you think the case is going blank on you? Look, Miss Jane,
I've drawn exactly nothing all the way down the line. Nobody sent this telegram to you. Nobody committed the
murders. Nobody knows anything about anything. I'm up
a tree."

I poured him some coffee and added the fixings the way
he liked them, and cut a good-sized hunk of gingerbread
and took another slice for myself. It might have been better with whipped cream instead of plain apple sauce, but
I doubt it.

When Burke had gotten himself outside of half a loaf
of gingerbread and a couple of cups of coffee, he looked a
little better, and dallied with some apple-sauce and a third
cup of coffee.

He was still sitting there, with the last cup of coffee
half gone, when Curly the cop stuck his head in at the

door and gasped: "Come quick, sir. Here's another murder."

"While I sat and ate gingerbread," said Burke. And before I could say another word, he was out of the door and
halfway up the stairs.

12

It was only fifteen minutes after that when I was really accused of murder, and how I escaped being actually arrested I still don't know. The evidence was all clearly pointing in my direction. Just look at the way I had thrown away the other half of the gingerbread I'd given Dulcy. True, it hadn't been thrown far, but then, as Curly put in, with indignation: "How was she going to know that anybody'd eat the gingerbread right away instead of waiting until suppertime and after that the rest of the garbage might have been emptied?"

It seems terrible, even to think of it. But it was true.

The gingerbread that I had given Dulcy was poisoned.

And I had done it myself, with my own hands. At least they said so.

I escaped being arrested and charged with murder only because Burke talked the rest of them into the notion that there was a slight element of doubt because the bottle of almond extract had disappeared and I hadn't left the room at all, and because I hadn't completely destroyed the rest of the cake but had tossed it into my little painted garbage can and neatly covered it after I had spilled the vinegar on it.

They didn't believe me when I told about the ping outside that had made me nervous. It wasn't until afterwards that I remembered hearing exactly that same sound earlier, down in the cellar when Burke and I were getting the jam and the peaches.

The fact of the poisoned gingerbread was so terrible that it drove everything else out of my mind.

Burke said: "Poison. And she's been eating gingerbread—your gingerbread! Why didn't you tell me that you made two different kinds of it—or did you?"

"But I ate it myself—and you did, Mr. Burke. We ate almost the whole loaf. And it's exactly the same mixture as in the other loaf—honestly it is. I made it all together in my big bowl. The same molasses, the same flour, the same soda and sugar—everything the same, except the vanilla. Why, I just mixed up the whole batch together for the two loaves and then divided it and added different flavorings to the two halves, as an experiment, before I poured the batter into the pan."

I just had to make him believe me. And somehow I felt that he did, to a degree. "Give me the flavorings, Miss Jane. Obviously there is nothing wrong with the one you used in the cake you and I ate. But give it to me, anyhow—both of them, both bottles. What was the other flavoring?"

"There was vanilla in the cake that you and I ate. And there was almond flavoring in the cake I gave Dulcy. Is she dead, Mr. Burke? Did I kill her? I don't know how I could. This was the same flavoring I used for a pudding last week, and I ate it myself and it didn't hurt me."

"Almond. I knew it. And I let it get past me when we searched the room. Where was it?"

"Right here on the shelf with all the rest of my supplies. See, I have flour and sugar and cereal, salt and pepper and spices, all sorts of flavors, orange and lemon, vanilla and raspberry. At home I always made cakes with different flavors for the different layers. My little brother likes them."

"You didn't tell me that you had a little brother. You said that you were all alone," snapped Burke.

"I'm all alone here in town. At home in Bridgeport I have two brothers, one older than I am and one younger. The older one got married about eight or nine months ago, and when I came here six months ago, he took the kid brother to live with him, to give me a chance to see the world." I was almost in tears, although even then I wasn't the kind of a person who relies on tears to relieve emotion.

"Well, you've seen the world, all right." Burke was grim. "Maybe you'll see how it looks from behind the bars. Look, Miss Jane, there's every reason to suppose that you're guilty of these murders. I could build up a case like nobody's business. It would be pretty and neatly tied with pink ribbons. But somehow I can't help feeling that it's as much news to you as it is to me. Maybe I'm just influenced by the fact that you're little and pretty, but I don't think so. I've seen prettier murderers in my day. Maybe it's the coffee at odd hours that got me. We'll take a chance on you, anyhow, but don't go out of this house for the next few days if you can help it, and I'm going to live here myself, practically, in between times, and keep somebody else here whenever I'm not."

All through this long speech he kept me standing in front of him like a kid getting a scolding before the teacher spanks him.

And we were just at that point when Riley came dashing in, as green around the gills as a boy who had eaten too many green apples.

He grabbed at my arm. "What happened, Jane?"

"Dulcy's dead. I poisoned her. With gingerbread!"

Burke started to say something, and I realized later what it was, but he changed his mind and just listened.

"Impossible. You're not a murderer. Listen, Burke, you're not thinking that this girl did anything like that.

Look at her. She's the very picture of innocence. She couldn't harm a fly."

His red cockade of hair stood up, and he pounded on Burke's shoulder as if he needed to emphasize his points with brawn and vigor.

"I've been trying to tell him, Riley, and I think," I said hopefully, my eyes on Burke, "that he believes me a little."

"Come into your room again," Burke said, and the three of us were back where we had started from. Systematically Burke went on a thorough search, talking as he went, asking minute questions about where things had been. He took the can with the debris of baking in it without even opening it. He moved everything on the shelf carefully, using some thin rubber gloves he took out of his pocket and handling the stuff gingerly and putting everything back exactly where it was.

"And nobody ever touches these shelves except you, to take things off?" he asked, finally, taking off the gloves.

"That's true," I told him, while Riley sat on the arm of a chair with all the suspense of a plane about to take off. Then I remembered one thing—something terribly important.

"Wait, Mr. Burke. When Dulcy was in the room a while ago, when she came in to ask me to go into the beauty shop business with her after I got my money—"

"What's that?" snapped Burke.

I repeated it: "Dulcy came into my room just now to ask me to go into the beauty shop business with her after I got my money."

"But didn't you call upstairs and ask her and the Johnson girl to come down here to get some of your gingerbread?" There was something peculiar about his voice.

"No. I just baked the gingerbread because I didn't have anything else to do and you told me to stay in my room till you got back, Mr. Burke. Remember? I thought that we could eat it with coffee later the next time you got hungry."

"And you didn't bake it with any special intention of giving any to Dulcy?"

"No. She was the last person I'd have offered it to. I don't like her much. I suppose that I oughtn't to tell you this, because she's dead and you think I killed her, but I honestly didn't bake it for her. It was only because I felt ashamed of my lack of hospitality that I called after her and handed up the cake to her, on the stairs."

My nerves tingled and I felt that I needed a warning to walk warily, but somehow Mr. Burke was working on the side of justice and I wanted to help him.

I wondered then why I had ever thought that things ought to be kept from the police for private reasons of my own, and I didn't realize that this confidence that Burke inspired in me was the same thing that brought him success in all of his cases—or almost all.

When the newspapers panned him during the next few days for being right there so many times when the murderer struck, he didn't say a word in his own defense. He just went on in the same casual fashion, tying up the loose ends and trying to get reasonable answers to reasonable questions.

Reporters were hard. I've mentioned already the day that I spent with policemen and reporters practically under my feet all the time, and that other hour when Riley had saved me from terror at their hands, but I think that I was almost as resentful for Burke as I was for myself. After all, the reason why they panned him most was because he said he thought that there wasn't enough evidence for a case against me. Riley told me of a session Burke had had with the chief of police and the D. A., but that was later.

"So the giving of the gingerbread was a gesture to soften your refusal?" Burke asked.

"But I didn't refuse. I said that I wasn't sure that I was going to get the money, but if I did I'd think very seriously about Dulcy's beauty shop."

Riley sat up straight, and Burke came toward me and took both of my hands and looked straight into my eyes. "You didn't refuse? You told her that you might accept?"

"Yes. Didn't she tell you—?" Then I thought that I'd forgotten that my gingerbread had poisoned Dulcy. "Then ask the Johnson girl. She heard it. She'll tell you."

"Did you really mean to go into business with her?"

"No. I didn't," I answered frankly. "It was just that I thought I'd better keep on good terms with her, and I could stall along until the worst of this was over."

The ghost of a grin came over Burke's face, and his voice was almost casual again for a few minutes.

"Tell me the rest. What happened after she asked you and you gave her the answer? Don't leave out anything. Tell me every step. What did she say, and what did you say? And did the Johnson girl say anything?"

"The Johnson girl said," I recalled, "only one thing. That she wanted to rest, that she didn't feel well because she'd eaten too much fish for lunch or something like that. I can't remember the exact words."

"What? Say that again. She didn't feel well because she ate too much fish for lunch. You're sure?"

"I'm sure. Then Dulcy said she'd better take some bicarbonate of soda, and she walked over to this supply shelf and took my baking soda off the shelf. I couldn't refuse, very well. You'll find it in her room, probably, and the Johnson girl will tell you the same thing I do. Besides, the soda's all right. That isn't poisoned. I used it in the cake you and I ate, too, Mr. Burke. And you don't feel sick, do you?"

"Just sick of murder," Burke said. "Could Dulcy have touched anything else on the shelf? Are you sure that the almond flavoring was there at the time? Could she have taken it herself?"

I thought hard. "She could have taken it, but why should she? Besides, she wouldn't know it was poisoned, if it really was, and I didn't see how it could be."

"And if she did know it was poisoned, then when did the poison get into it and did she have anything to do with that?" put in Riley.

"It's all so impossible," I wailed. "The flavoring couldn't be poisoned. I've eaten stuff I made with it. And yet the only way that Dulcy could have been poisoned by the cake was to have the poison in the almond flavor, because that was the only thing different from the flavor I used on your cake, Mr. Burke."

"Unless somebody could have come in and added poison to it or substituted bottles. Was there any mention made at all of almond flavoring in the gingerbread, Miss Jane?"

"None at all. It was a crazy idea. I never put any kind of extra flavor at all in my gingerbread, but I just felt like experimenting, and that was a quick way. I guess that I was bored with the idea of staying in one room all day with nothing special to do."

Burke looked incredulous at the idea of being bored in the middle of a murder case, but it was true. "Anyhow," I went on, "we didn't mention the word 'flavoring' or the word 'gingerbread' at all until after the girls had left the room, and I just asked them if they wanted gingerbread and didn't mention the flavoring. Besides, I didn't remember which I had put almond in and which vanilla, so it was just chance that made me grab one or the other. It's just chance that I'm not dead, and you, Mr. Burke, instead of Dulcy, if the flavoring was really poisoned by somebody. And if Miss Johnson hadn't been eating too much fish for

lunch so she felt bad, she might have been eating gingerbread, too, and they'd both be dead instead of one of
them."

Burke looked a little odd. "That's true," he said faintly,
remembering, no doubt, the huge hunk of gingerbread he
had managed to put away himself. I haven't made gingerbread since, and I'd like to bet that Mr. Burke hasn't eaten it.

"No real murderer would be such a little fool, Burke.
Admit that," demanded Riley, and to my amazement,
Burke nodded.

"Either she's as innocent as that marble mantelpiece,
or she's as guilty as any mass murderer I ever saw. I think
she's innocent. God knows whether I can keep her out of
jail long enough to prove it."

I've been thinking, lately, about all of these points.
Time and time again they asked me questions about the
shelf and the baking and the gingerbread, and how I happened to do such an outlandish thing as use almond flavor
in gingerbread. I couldn't give them any sensible answer
because there wasn't any. It's just one of those silly things
that cooks do without any reason at all. Most of the cooking geniuses do it, and most of the cooking messes are
made with the same type of experimentation.

That all came later. Then I was still swept with horror
at the idea of Dulcy lying up in her room with all that
vain beauty made futile forever, with all of her coquetry
dead. And all because of something put into a cake that I
had made.

But we were still standing there, all three of us, with
our hearts heavy—at least mine was—when there came a
little knock on the door, and into the room came—Dulcy!

Dulcy—alive and well! Not the ghost of a girl but the
girl herself, as alive and vital as she had been a short time
before in this same room. And she pointed a bright-nailed
finger at me and said: "Murderer!"

And then she just stood there, in the middle of my room, and let out the loudest series of shrieks I had ever heard from her.

Dulcy was not dead.

13

I lost what little sense I had left and could only stand there, pointing at Dulcy as she pointed at me. Now that I look back at it we must have looked very funny to anybody looking on—if there had been anybody except Riley and Burke, who were almost as upset as we were.

"But you're dead!" I told Dulcy finally, in a tone as stupid as any I've ever used.

"Kay Johnson's dead. And you killed her. You gave me that poisoned gingerbread. I didn't eat it, but Kay did, and she died in agony."

So that was the explanation. The Johnson girl had eaten the cake instead of Dulcy. And the wrong girl was dead. Here again death was such a chancy thing, as a neighbor of mine in Bridgeport used to say. The wrong flavoring. One loaf of gingerbread and not the other. The wrong girl eating the cake. Or was it the wrong girl? Had the murderer decided that I might bake and give the cake to Dulcy, who would give it to Miss Johnson? No, that was too deliberately involved to be believed. This death wasn't murder. It was an accident. Surely they couldn't think it was anything else.

"Dulcy, tell Mr. Burke that you took the flavoring," I begged. "Tell him that when you took the baking soda you took the flavoring, too. Then he can analyze it and can show that there isn't any poison in it. Honestly, Dulcy, I didn't poison her. Why, I don't even know the girl," I appealed.

"You know me," said Dulcy flatly, "and it was me you wanted to kill. You were afraid that I'd tell what I know about your other murders."

"But, Dulcy—"

"Dulcy—" she mocked—"Dulcy. You can be plenty sweet to me when you want something, but you can't see me when you don't. They'll take you to jail and then you'll burn."

I was such an ignoramus that I didn't know what she was talking about. To me a burn was what you got on your hand when you took a hot pan out of the oven with too small a potholder. "Burn?"

"The electric chair, I mean," she announced calmly. That's what happens to murderers. You killed Miss Lizzie, and then you killed my Henry and Madame Terracci and Torry and now Bill Broad and Kay Johnson. That's enough to make you sit six times in the electric chair, but once will be enough," she added in triumph.

Burke and Riley were silent. I had a notion then, and I was probably right, that Burke wanted us to fight it out, thinking that he might learn something he needed from one of us.

"But Torry—and Bill Broad—" I started to say that they weren't dead yet, because so far as I knew they weren't.

Or were they dead by now? I hadn't seen Betty since the inquest on Madame Terracci, and soon there would be other inquests, other autopsies, and I'd be the central figure, splashed with a terrible spotlight. And Bill had been near death when I had seen him.

Did she really feel that I, an eighteen-year-old girl, could have done these murders? Even without Broad and Torry there were four deaths now—four murders. It was far more likely that some man from the outside had done the murders. "There's George—have you thought of George?" I begged Burke. "He has disappeared. Is he hiding somewhere in the house? Has he been seen at all? There are the attics and the cellars. We may have heard him—somebody may have seen him. Hunt for him—he may be the one."

"George is dead!" announced Dulcy flatly. "You killed him, too, so you could blame him for all the rest of the murders."

"Tell him what you did with the flavoring," I begged Dulcy.

"What flavoring?" asked Dulcy, and then I knew that she wasn't going to help me at all. But if she hadn't taken it, where could it be?

"You're the only one who went near the shelves, since I used it in the gingerbread. If anybody took that bottle of almond flavoring, you did, Dulcy!" I was pleading for my life, it seemed to me then, but Dulcy was granite and steel.

"I don't know anything about any flavoring. I did borrow some baking soda from you for Kay Johnson. She took it a little while before she died, I think, but that wasn't what killed her. It was the poison you put in the gingerbread for me."

Burke came in then. "Miss Dulcy—you know how important this is? You wouldn't lie about the flavoring? You know that it's life and death for Miss Jane here."

"It was life and death for Kay Johnson, too. I didn't see any of your flavoring. I didn't touch a thing in your room except the plain box of baking soda, and that was right here on the shelf."

I had put it away—or had I? But there wasn't any place for it to be except on the table or in the cupboard on the shelf. "If it was here and nobody came in but you, then you must have taken it."

"Or else—listen, Mr. Burke, maybe she threw it out of the window. Did you think of that?" asked Dulcy.

Maybe I'm stupid, but it would never have occurred to me to get rid of anything that way. Look at the ashes from the telegram. I could have scattered those out of the window, and I didn't even think of it. There are people who throw things out of windows and other people who don't. I even knew a woman back in Bridgeport who threw her dishwater out of the window instead of pouring it down the sink.

"I doubt it, but we'll look on the street, in the gutter." Burke went to the door and gave a few directions to a policeman in the hall. Then he came back and sat down.

Those minutes before the time that Burke gave the orders and the time that the policeman came in with the bottle were the longest I've ever spent. When Dulcy had suggested that I might have thrown the bottle out of the window I'd been certain that nobody would believe her. But there was some special reason why she'd suggested it. Would it have been possible for Dulcy herself to take the bottle and throw it out of the window? Was it possible that the "ping" I'd heard was the sound of a little bottle breaking on the gutter or the sidewalk. Was there an upstairs window out of which Dulcy could have thrown the stuff? And if she had done it, was it simply to throw suspicion on me?

The little bottle was broken. But through some chance there were a few drops of liquid left in the part of the bottle that was still whole. The pieces were all there, or most of them. The cop had put them in a box, and he held them out to Burke with the air of a woman giving some bad meat back to the butcher.

Dulcy turned to Burke with an air of triumph. "There, I told you she threw it out of the window." And I said, at almost the same minute:

"That must have been the noise I heard—the bottle breaking outside."

Burke, handling the box on which the glass and the bottle had been put, studied the liquid carefully, sniffing oddly at the smell.

There was something wrong with the color of the flavoring, I thought. Then I went closer, too, and looked without touching. The smell of the bitter almonds was much more pungent than it had been before. Yet the bottle was exactly the same. There was the spot of egg-yolk that I had spattered on the label.

"This was my bottle," I told Burke. "But the stuff in it has been changed. My flavoring wasn't that color. And it didn't smell that way. It was just a very faint almond smell. This smells like the inside of peach stones. It's much stronger."

Burke said sharply: "Are you sure, Miss Jane? The bottle is the same? How do you know? Any distinguishing mark?"

"That spot of egg yolk. And a policeman could probably find my fingerprints on it. But the stuff isn't what I used just now. I'd know it, honestly. Look, Mr. Burke. If this wasn't in the bottle when I made the almond-flavored gingerbread, then the gingerbread isn't poisoned. I'm sure it isn't. Have you analyzed it?"

"It was all eaten. A P.M. is being made now. But we'll test the gingerbread in the can, the part you spilled vinegar on. That will tell us."

For a wonder Burke looked suddenly hopeful, as if he saw a way out of the dilemma. "There's a chance," he said, "that the poison was added afterwards, after the bottle was taken from your room. That puts it pretty well up to you, Miss Dulcy, if you took the bottle."

"But I didn't take the bottle. Jane must have thrown it out of the window. I swear she did. It would be just like her. And then she'd blame me."

"But if the poison wasn't in the gingerbread, then how did Kay Johnson die?" I found myself asking. "Look, Mr. Burke. She was sick when she came here. Maybe she was poisoned then, by the fish. Maybe the gingerbread didn't have anything to do with it, or the bottle either. Where did she eat the fish?"

"Out of a can. We had salad made of canned salmon. It was perfectly good," Dulcy reported. "Kay made it the way she likes it, and maybe she did eat too much of it. She was a little greedy. But I ate it, too, and it didn't hurt me, so it was all right. She's just trying to draw attention from herself. Kay didn't say she was sick when she came down with me. She said she was tired. And if she had been sick, how could she have eaten gingerbread the way she did when she came upstairs?"

"I'm afraid that Dulcy's right on one thing, Mr. Burke," I remembered. "Miss Johnson did say that she was tired, not that she was sick. But she looked sick."

"We'll know soon. A P.M. should tell us more of what we want to know," said Burke grimly.

I didn't know then that a P.M. was a post-mortem, but there wasn't any way in which my gingerbread could have been poisoned if the flavoring was all right. And somehow I knew that it had been. Because color and flavor were different from what they had been at the time I baked the gingerbread.

"Listen, Mr. Burke, where did you put the can that I threw the cake in?" I asked, a crazy idea forming in my head.

"Here, next to the door." He nodded his head toward the pail. I walked over, and I knew that they were all watching me as I opened the can with the foot press. Right on top was the cake, still in the wax paper that had lined the cake pan. It didn't smell of gingerbread or of almond. It smelled of the vinegar I had spilled on it. Without touching it, I bent over to study it carefully. It seemed to me that one corner of it had escaped the vinegar and had been protected by the wax paper from the sides of the can, which were perfectly clean anyhow, because I always used paper bags and scalded out the can every day. It's the only way to do in one-room apartments where you entertain your guests in the same room that houses your garbage can.

"If that cake is all right, then you'll know that I'm innocent," I said to Burke, and he nodded, although Dulcy still looked supercilious.

I grabbed at one corner of the cake that was clean of vinegar, and before Burke or anybody else could stop me, I had the cake in my mouth.

It was melodramatic, of course, and I'm not usually a melodramatic person. But if the stuff was all right then they wouldn't suspect me of murder, and if it was not all right and they wanted to send me to the electric chair for murders that I didn't do, I didn't want to live anyhow.

I didn't eat the gingerbread with relish. It smelled of vinegar, even if it didn't taste vinegary. The almond wasn't at all evident. I couldn't taste or smell it at all, not even as much as I had tasted the hint of vanilla in the other loaf of cake. There couldn't be any poison in it, although I waited for a few minutes in order to feel symptoms. I won't say that I wasn't afraid, because I was. I was scared to death. But it was easier to be scared than to spend the next days not knowing whether I would be sent to jail and maybe killed for murder when I hadn't done it at all.

Of course if I had had any sense, I'd have waited until the cake was analyzed, knowing that no power would find poison in it if my flavoring hadn't been poisoned. But I couldn't think of that then. I did that silly melodramatic thing and I've never really been sorry. It's probably the only really brave thing I've ever done in my life. Certainly it's the only reckless thing, and every girl ought to have one reckless bit of courage to look back on after she's a grandmother or an old maid, even if it's only doing a silly thing because she thinks she is saving her own life.

I don't know how quickly a person would die after eating poisoned gingerbread, but I do know that an hour later I was still safe and sound, sitting in my own room after all the excitement.

I didn't feel any the worse for the whole business, except for my thinking of that poor Miss Johnson who would never be alive again.

Riley had a grand byline story in the *Standard,* all about my "heroic act to prove my innocence," but when I look at the faded clippings today they strike me as a pretty silly bit of melodrama that wasn't at all necessary.

Several things came out during the next few days. In the first place we learned that "Kay Johnson" and Dulcy were really sisters, which astonished us all. Then Bill Broad didn't die, but lingered on as an interesting invalid, and when he finally came down in a slightly languid air and a brocaded bathrobe, looked like the handsome hero of a hospital drama.

I was grateful that so handsome a man hadn't got himself murdered. Not that I was in love with him, or anything like that, but he was plenty handsome.

Kay, like Henry and Madame Terracci, had died of one of the prussic acid type poisons. I wouldn't try, at this late date, to give details, but I do remember something about the quickness of the action of the poison, and the odd fact that it smelled like bitter almond flavoring only more so. The newspapers seemed to make a big fuss over the fact that Miss Lizzie had died from some sort of phosphorus poisoning while the rest had all died of much the same prussic acid type of poison. Some of the sob sisters seemed to think that this indicated a different murderer.

One paper put out big headlines about Smith. He had once been a detective, it seems, who had been mixed up in some kind of a racket and had been dismissed. Because of that one year of detective experience he considered himself an expert on any sort of police procedure, as well as on almost anything else you could mention. One of the columnists got hold of Riley's name for him, "Cahoots" Smith, and they played the idea ragged, and sent Mr. Smith fuming around the house, muttering to himself under his breath. Nobody had an alibi for any of the murders, so far as we could tell, because all of them were the type that might have occurred some time after the murderer had gone safely to his bed.

Poisoned chocolates for all of them except Kay, and they were never quite sure about her. They found the poison and the gingerbread, but there was no way of being certain whether the poison was in the gingerbread, except for my foolhardy stunt of tasting the stuff myself. Dulcy and a susceptible reporter, working together, put forward a beautiful idea that part of the gingerbread was free from poison and the rest poisoned, and that I had given Dulcy the poisoned part but had eaten the other part.

Like Snow White again. Remember the apple that was half good and half poison? And of course nobody believed the idea. Elaborate ideas make good headlines but little sense.

All through those days Burke kept hold of the filigree button from my desk that had been found under the box of poisoned candy in Madame Terracci's room.

We were all sitting tight, holding onto the remnants of our sanity and still trying to make headway, when my brothers descended on me, both of them, from Bridgeport.

Burke and Riley were there, drinking coffee, but not eating gingerbread, when the door opened and in walked my two brothers.

"We've come," announced my big brother, "to take you home with us."

14

I had almost forgotten what it was like to have a family. I hadn't written them anything about all this, hoping that they'd miss the big town headlines. After all, we have mostly local news in the Bridgeport *Weekly*.

But the police decided to follow up the case back home to see whether I'd left a poison trail in Bridgeport, too, and the darlings came, all armed with protective manners and advice, and if you've never had advice from brothers, then you've never had advice.

Even the kid, aged sixteen, was primed with arguments about the big city being no place for a small-town girl who wants to stay out of the headlines.

Just to quiet them, after Burke and Riley and the rest had gone and left us alone, I brought out the Christmas presents that I had for them, although it wasn't nearly Christmas. Anyhow, unbirthday and un-Christmas presents are much more fun, besides serving now and then to cast aside bones of contention.

I had carefully rewrapped in its red tissue paper and silver ribbons the electric torch that had played so important a part in my life on the night of the first murders when the lights went out. And when Bud lit up his pipe and savored the first of the new tobacco that had been so carefully blended, I remembered back to the night when

I had considered giving pipe and tobacco to Riley so his venomous pipe and horrible tobacco wouldn't profane my room.

The one-room apartment in which we sat was so different from the chintzy little cottage at home that I had trouble in adjusting my brothers to the place. But as usual, a meal set us all at ease. I had been a little hesitant about baking since my trouble with the gingerbread. But Burke had had all the supplies carted away for testing and I bought new ones, and Riley had put a safe lock on the cabinet. So I went right along preparing waffles and brought out some orange syrup that I'd put up to go with waffles. I could tell from my first sight of any stuff I'd put up whether anybody had touched it. I used a special kind of jar lid that made a vacuum seal on everything except preserves and jelly, and on those I used the paraffine with string arrangement about which I had told Burke earlier, so I knew that the stuff was absolutely free from tampering and safe to use.

As the fragrance of the waffles began to spread through the room, my brothers stopped putting forth arguments and began to eat, and I was able to do the talking and present my point of view to an audience with its mouth full of food. That has been the most effective way of exerting woman's influence for centuries. It beats nagging all hollow. Wait till he gets his mouth full and then talk.

At any rate, Bud, my older brother, was persuaded by the time his fourth waffle had vanished, but it took five waffles to influence Butch, my younger brother. Young people are always so conservative, I thought, from the eminence of my own eighteen years.

It seems, as I discovered when I stopped baking waffles, that all Bridgeport was worried about me. They were ordering big town newspapers every day and sitting for hours consulting about me. They had made up their mind

that I was to get out of this house and come home where
I belonged and it was up to Bud to make me come. They
worked on Tess, Bud's wife, and she in turn worked on Bud,
who had had the odd notion that I should be left alone to
work out my own salvation, because if I had wanted help
I'd have written home for it.

And Butch had come along because the influence of the
chee-ild might be effective. The child was almost a foot
taller than I, and looked some five years older, in spite of
the fact that I was two years his senior.

Butch was hardest to persuade. He had had his ideas
handed to him, full-fledged, by Mrs. Harrison, the president of the Community Club in Bridgeport. I should settle down at home and get acquainted again with all of my
old friends.

I should lose all my city habits (I hadn't really grown
any in six months, I told Butch, but he didn't believe me).
I read between the lines that Mrs. Harrison intended me
eventually to marry her nincompoop of a nephew, but she
hadn't told Butch that. She'd mentioned it to me often
enough at home, not knowing much about the little nitwit
from the ten-cent store with whom her nephew had been
in love for years.

Butch wavered a little when I mentioned the legacy
from Madame Terracci. "You wouldn't take it," he said
with great scorn, but I said that there wasn't anybody left
in Madame Terracci's family to get it, and she had said in
this letter left with the will that the reason it had been
left to me was that I had been kind to her. She had left
something to Betty, too, because Betty had been kind as
well, but there was quite a lot of the legacy, jewels and
bonds and things that I'd probably get eventually, when
they made up their minds that I didn't have anything to
do with the deaths.

"I earned enough this summer for a bicycle," Butch said finally, "but I had to sell it to get enough for tuition at school. And even that wasn't quite enough. It'd be kind of nice to have some cash in this family for a change."

"It's Jane's, not yours," Bud told him quickly.

It didn't take much time, though, to persuade the boys that if I got the legacy it would be used to make things easier for all of us. "And that would be much more fun," I finished, "then using it to start a beauty shop with Dulcy."

The only reason I mention this in detail was because, at the moment when I said this last thing about Dulcy and the beauty shop, I looked at the window, where I thought that I heard a tiny noise.

And there, looking in and listening to what I said, was Dulcy on the little balcony outside the window. She was gone before I got sense enough to get up and go to the window. But I know that she must have heard my last sentence, which meant that I had now let her know that she had nothing to expect from me when I got the legacy and that there was therefore no reason why she shouldn't do her spiteful best to get me arrested.

Now that I think of it, she hadn't been any too gentle to me even when she thought she'd get the money. But that was to be expected, because that was the way Dulcy acted with women anyhow. Some girls do.

And now that Kay Johnson was dead—

We spent the next few minutes in going over and over the points that hadn't appeared in the newspapers. The most astonishing thing to me was why these two girls had stayed together when they were so different and when they didn't even want it known that they were sisters. Burke hadn't been able to get any reason for this out of Dulcy. She did say that Johnson was the family name and that her own real name was Dora, but that she had changed to her fancy name as a sort of nom de stage. I'm not responsible for that silly word, Dulcy is.

We all kept on calling her Dulcy, which was much more fitted to her than Dora. Although, come to think of it, doesn't Dora mean "gift"? And that was what she was fondest of, and didn't get nothing else but, as Florian Slappey might say.

Butch and Bud went back home that night, still protesting, but their visit gave me a self-confidence I had lost. Also, it made me conscious of several things that I'd almost forgotten. Telling them about facts made them more definite in my mind, too.

For one thing, Butch made me think of Henry's ghost on the night of the storm at the time the lights were out. I had passed it off as a figment of Mrs. Meyer's imagination, although I had to confess that it was almost the only sign I'd seen that she had an imagination.

Of course Dulcy saw the ghost too, but Dulcy is the kind who'd agree to any lie for the sake of sharing the spotlight.

But if Mrs. Meyer saw something, there was something to see. Therefore, somewhere in the house was a man who could have appeared in the doorway of that dark room on that night and could have made Mrs. Meyer think that he was Henry. Now who could it be? I couldn't swear to the presence that night of any of the people in the house except Mrs. Meyer and Dulcy, who had talked so I heard them at the moment the supposed ghost was seen. The rest of the people in the room might have been going and coming all of the time, for all I knew. Then there was the figure that had brushed past me on the stairs. Maybe that had been my imagination, too, however, since I was scared to death going downstairs in the dark. I've never been especially fond of stairs since the time I broke my ankle and it was so hard to go up them on crutches.

Mrs. Meyer had seen other things, too. She saw me on the stairs that night when I went to let in Broad. But I hadn't gone upstairs. I hadn't gone any further than the door. She had also seen Torry coming out of Miss Lizzie's door at eight o'clock that evening when nobody else had seen him in the house for days. This last was undoubtedly true, because Betty's evidence was the same. But how had she seen me when I hadn't been there, and how had she seen Henry when Henry was dead? I mention these points here because they turned out to be important later on.

There was one more thing about Mrs. Meyer that I kept remembering, and that was the way that she and Bill Broad had looked at each other when Riley or Burke asked whether there was any connection between Henry and Miss Lizzie. And right after that, both of them had looked oddly at Mr. Smith and Madame Terracci. This last might have been entirely without meaning. I didn't know. But if I could get Mrs. Meyer or Broad to tell Burke what they knew about any connection between Miss Lizzie and Henry, we might get to the bottom of these murders and know something about why the persons had been chosen apparently at random from the household. Now that Broad had probably been thoroughly frightened by his own narrow escape from death, he ought to tell what he knew. The next time the murderer might be more successful.

And what connection was there between Madame Terracci and Cahoots Smith, if any? And did Broad and Mrs. Meyer know about it?

When Burke came in the next day, upset by the fact that the Chief of Police had threatened to take him off the case if he didn't show results soon, I mentioned these facts to him.

To my amazement, he was furious, too furious to be casual. "If you'd keep your pretty nose out of what doesn't concern you," he said, "and stop balling up a smooth case,

I'd make some headway. Look how you mussed things up with the gingerbread stuff and the way the headlines panned me when you did your poison-eating stunt. I had a right to arrest you when I first had the evidence of that filigree button, and why I don't do it I'm sure I don't know. But stay where you're told to stay so I don't get sent out to Mt. Eden to patrol a beat next week."

"I've got a job," I reminded him, wondering whether I'd get fired for prolonging my two days' holiday to a week more.

"You had a job." Burke sounded grim and resentful. "Your boss talked to me yesterday and told me he was giving you a week's salary in lieu of notice because he couldn't afford to keep a stenographer who got mixed up in police cases."

Well, there went my job. "You've got the legacy," Burke reminded me. "It'll be a while before you get it, but you could go home to Bridgeport. Your brothers told me that they'd take care of you. And I'll—" He stopped, and I wasn't sure for a while what he meant to say, because he sidetracked himself on a different subject.

"While we're alone," he began, "has it ever struck you that there was any thing the least suspicious about Riley? We can't omit anybody, you know. I've gone through my periods of suspecting you, too, although your last bit of tomfoolery pretty well cured me of that, that and your good cooking."

"Riley's swell. He has dragged the reporters off me when they were screaming for the kill."

"But that may have been in order to keep all the best stories for himself. And believe you me," Burke added earnestly, "there have been enough good stories in this house in the last week or two to satisfy the script writer of a radio serial! All that we need now are a fire and a flood."

He was optimistic, only he didn't know it then because our troubles were far from over.

"Riley is just a newspaper cub who intends to be a by-line man if this murder gives him a chance," I said, with all the oratory of a girl who isn't quite sure of what she's talking about because she doesn't know the vocabulary.

"And you're sure," suggested Burke casually but carefully, "that he didn't start the whole business from the beginning and then keep the ball rolling for the sake of making himself a sought-after reporter instead of only a kid on part-time routine fill-ins?"

The idea was absolutely new to me. I remembered how different Riley had become just as soon as the murders began, and how we all looked up to him and waited for him to tell us what to do because he alone knew.

"He—Smith was right when he said he saw Riley cutting the telephone wire that night, Mr. Burke."

I felt like a traitor. "I—I saw something shiny in his hand—a scissors or a knife, probably. And I was never quite sure how that telephone business got straightened out, that night. It was all so mixed up. How many times were the police called?"

"That's a question that we'll discuss later." Burke seemed doubtful, and I wasn't to know until the case was entirely over that he hadn't had a call at all. I want to put down here the facts of the telephone incident here so that it's straight.

The way that the police came without being called was this: The electric lights went out in several houses on our street, and one house called the police, saying that there was a prowler in the attic. That was next door to us. The prowler, by the way, was never found, so his apparent presence was probably just a creation of the storm and the fear that the darkness and the lightning brought.

The police checked our house to make sure that the prowler hadn't been there, and when they were told, at the door, about the murders, one of the policemen had gone

back to the precinct station to report the murders and set
all machinery in motion.

It all sounds terribly involved, and even when I had
heard every detail, Burke had to explain it to me again.
"At no time during that night did anybody call the police
from this house."

"But Riley called—using your name. He said Burke. I
heard him distinctly. And then you came."

"I came because it was my job to come. Riley used my
name because it's probably the only name on the homicide
squad that he remembered."

"And Bill Broad called—twice." I explained that first
call with the blood-sticky dime I had found in my bathrobe pocket and the way that Bill Broad had borrowed a
nickel from Riley for the second call that Broad had made.

I was all at sea again. Because if Bill Broad and Riley
had both lied, then I didn't know what to believe. And Bill
Broad was out, as a murderer. He was completely in the
clear because he had himself just escaped being murdered.

And that left Riley in a very suspicious place. It didn't
sound likely that any man would murder just for the sake of
getting himself a reputation as a good reporter with exciting stories to tell. But then murder has never seemed a reasonable pastime to me, any more than bridge or crocheting.

The trouble with me, as I saw later, was that I didn't
seem to be able to string facts together and make any sort
of real connection between them.

But I wasn't the only one. Even Burke had trouble with
this case.

And just as Burke and I sat sulkily eyeing the last cup
of coffee and wondering what in the world we were going to do about Riley, in came Riley—with his crest of
red hair and the eager youth in his eyes, and immediately
I took heart. Because a man who looked like that could
never be a murderer.

15

"Well, boys and girls," Riley sang out cheerfully, "we've got us a story."

"Well, little boy," said Burke casually, "we've got us some murders. Know the word? It means people dead, and it frequently hurts to die. Did you know that, Riley? Don't take it so damned cheerfully."

"Don't you realize, Burke, that you've got to look at every case as a puzzle? Find the murderer. All clues final. Now let's look at this sensibly, Burke," Riley added. "These murders have happened, and there isn't anything, so far as I know, that I could have done to keep the folks from being murdered. Then why in the name of the Fourth Estate shouldn't I make the most of the fact that I'm right here on the scene and get myself a permanent job? Do you know how hard it is for a reporter to get a job today?"

He paused for dramatics. "I know," put in Burke meaningly, "how hard it will be for this policeman to get a job if you keep on throwing monkey wrenches in the machinery with your desire for bylines."

"Now don't be like that, Burke. Why shouldn't I? This is my big opportunity. You've made your name. I'm just a cub trying to get along in the world and here comes this big chance."

"And that," said Burke feelingly, "is why you cut the telephone wire on the night of the first murders so that nobody would call the police until you had a chance to solve the murders with your own genius for crime?"

"Of course." Riley was brazen. But was he telling the truth? Was this the only reason? Was he an opportunist— or a murderer? He was one or the other, and Burke obviously didn't know which. Neither did I, even when I looked at his audacious grin and his crest of red hair.

"Riley, of course you know that you aren't above suspicion yourself," put in Burke casually. Riley's eyes narrowed.

"Are you planning to put me behind bars?" he asked, almost as casually as Burke himself.

Burke watched him closely but didn't answer, while I just sat there, as stupid as my chair. I couldn't even tell, from their faces or their voices, whether Burke seriously suspected Riley or whether Riley was completely innocent except of the desire to solve a mystery before the police got there.

"Sit down, Riley," invited Burke, indicating the rocking chair. And I've thought, since, that rocking chair might be a good addition to police headquarters, because look how it puts people at a disadvantage to be rocking when serious questions are being asked. It's almost as disconcerting as to be on one of those low couches where you need a derrick to help you get up, even if you do weigh only ninety-five pounds.

"If you're not guilty, Riley, then you have a pet suspect," Burke said. "You are just as likely to be wrong as I am, but if you have a suspect and you're basing your information for newspaper use on facts that aren't in my possession, I swear that I'll keep you off of every newspaper staff in this town, and I have my own reasons for knowing most of the city editors."

Riley started stammering then. But since pleas didn't seem to do much good, he seemed to decide to go into action, handing out what little information he had. Now, you know when they broadcast foreign news how they remind you that the broadcast is originating in a government owned and operated station, subject to censorship at point of origin. In the same way I want to remind you that I had no way of knowing, any more than Burke, exactly how truthful Riley's remarks were. For all we knew, he was himself guilty, or, if innocent, was barking up the wrong tree.

"There are two men who have never been under suspicion at all in this case," Riley began, with as much dignity as anybody in a rocking chair can assume.

"If you mean George and Torry," Burke put in shortly, "we've considered them. But Torry has been unconscious during these last murders—unconscious, under guard, in a hospital most of the time. And George has been gone since that first night. It is possible that he, too, is dead, and his body will be found."

"I mean Cahoots Smith," corrected Riley, "and the mailman."

"The mailman. You mean Peregrine Roger?"

Come to think of it, I'd never heard the mailman's name before. I had never seen him, except that one time and at the inquests, in anything other than his blue uniform, with one shoulder fitted with the pad on which his bag would fit. To me he was simply "the mailman" and not a real person with a real name.

"Yes, if that's his name. Now look at him as a possibility for your murderer, Burke." Riley seemed excited. "He's a frustrated person. He studied for the ministry and didn't get to be what he wanted. Now he's a forgotten man. Nobody ever thinks of the mailman. They like or hate the things he brings, but he is only a tool, like a wheelbarrow

bringing fuel or a tin can holding food. Nobody notices
him. He is used to being unobtrusive. He could have gone
to any room in the house without comment from anybody,
because he is so colorless that nobody ever pays him any
attention."

"That may be right," Burke mentioned thoughtfully.

"True, we know nothing of his motive. But then there is
no real motive for these murders. So far as we can see, the
only things they have in common is that all of the people
were poisoned and that all of them lived in this house. Even
the poisons weren't all the same. True, all except one were
some form of prussic acid, but we have no evidence that the
poison was taken in the same way, in spite of the chocolates
that were beside some of the bodies. Am I right, Burke?"

"Y-e-es. In a way." Burke didn't seem certain.

"Because look at Broad. He swears that he didn't eat a
chocolate out of the box, that he never saw the box before.
His fingerprints aren't on it, and besides, he says that after
Madame Terracci he never wants to see a piece of chocolate
candy again. He says that the candy was a prop, put there
to make us think that he had been murdered that way."

Burke nodded. "I think he's right. When they washed
out his stomach they analyzed the residue, and there was
no sign of chocolate, although they found traces of the
poison. But why should the chocolates be there?"

"I'll bite. Why? But listen, Burke: we must look for
somebody who doesn't know that any P.M. would show
that the poisoned chocolates hadn't been used."

"That means that Smith is out. He was attached for a
year to the police department in his home town, but he
had too many handouts at the back doors of too many
interesting houses."

"Cahoots Smith was a detective. Therefore he knows
that the post mortem would show that chocolates hadn't
contained the poison," agreed Riley.

"Cahoots Smith was never a detective, except in his own conversation. Cahoots Smith (swell name for him, by the way, Riley) was a policeman in uniform, walking a beat in an out section of a suburb. Never anything more important than that, except in his own imagination."

"But a policeman would know about post mortems and probably a mailman wouldn't," explained Riley hopefully.

"A policeman might. And a mailman mightn't. But all of this is based on facts that are no facts. How do you know, Riley, that the murderer didn't know about the post mortems? Maybe the poisoned chocolates are some sort of symbol."

"Like a red star on a forehead or something like that? Something out of Edgar Wallace? Um—maybe."

"Then weren't any of the victims actually poisoned with the chocolates?" I asked that question myself, being too incredulous for further silence.

"A few," said Riley airily.

"Henry," added Burke, "died of prussic acid in almond chocolates from the factory where Madame Terracci worked. Then these others died of the same or similar poisons—except Miss Lizzie, who died of a form of phosphorus poisoning, which, by the way, is the reason for the luminous appearance of the skin, and the odd smell, like garlic. All of this was mentioned at the inquests. Weren't you interested enough to listen, Miss Jane?"

I was just too ignorant of the whole subject to know the meaning of what I heard. But it was all pretty straight now. As he went on, I even came to some realization of the many facts of any one murder investigation—and here there were so many murders, all mixed up.

Another odd thing was that there hadn't been a single funeral in the house in spite of all of the deaths. Madame Terracci hadn't had a family, and she had left directions for a private cremation, which looked a little suspicious to some of the police, because they thought that this sounded a little like suicide. But after all, she was alone in the world, and as she said in the note that was clipped on to her will in her top desk drawer:

"If there are any who remember me, I want them to think of me as I was in life. I don't want them to remember the details of my death."

Poor old woman. We were all to remember the details of her death long after most of us had forgotten her life in the tall house. But she couldn't know that then.

Henry's brother came on from his drugstore up state and took Henry's body back to his home town after the police had finished with it, and Betty had arranged a private burial for Aunt Lizzie to avoid some of the morbid sightseers who tried to mob the undertaking parlors.

As for Kay Johnson, who was so strangely Dulcy's sister, I don't know the rules of the etiquette, but it didn't seem quite right for me to go to her funeral when I was being accused of her murder.

All of this takes us far from the conversation between Riley and Burke. Riley wasn't quite certain whether the mailman or Cahoots Smith was the guilty man, although his hunch directed him toward the mailman, Peregrine Rogers. Such a name.

But how valuable this hunch was, I wasn't sure. Look how sure he'd been of Broad's guilt until Broad had gotten half-murdered himself. If Burke and I hadn't knocked on Broad's door at just the right minute, he'd be on the list of victims too.

Burke said slowly: "I can't feel that this mailman is important. We used all the routine methods of checking on him. He seems O.K., and there's no connection between him and any of the victims."

"What about Cahoots? Any connection?" queried Riley.

Burke shook his head. "Not much. He came from Centreville or some such place, a little burg not far from where

Miss Lizzie was brought up. He and Miss Lizzie and Madame Terracci were all about the same age, and we've managed to trace one period of about six months when they all lived in the same section, within a radius of some twenty miles, but that's the best we can do."

Riley brightened. "That's a lot. How's this? Lizzie and Cahoots were in love. They were twenty, maybe?"

"That's almost the age," admitted Burke. "Twenty-five, maybe."

"Riley, your hunch is good," Riley patted himself on the back. "Call it twenty-five. Lizzie and Cahoots are in love. They plan to get married. Along comes Terracci, then a beautiful singer with a foreign air and gorgeous glamor. She alienates Smith's affections and leaves Lizzie in the lurch. What about that?"

"But Lizzie was dead first. She wasn't the murderer of Terracci. Besides, that was many years ago, thirty or forty. And we have no way of knowing that they ever saw each other that long ago, even if they did live within twenty miles of each other." I wondered why Burke bothered to contradict Riley's pipedreams.

"So she was. Well, couldn't Cahoots have murdered Lizzie because she tried to renew the old love and then murdered Terracci because she was a disappointment after all these years?" Riley was the eternal optimist.

"Doesn't sound likely. No. We've tried all the standard methods of following them up. So far as we can tell, the three of them never knew each other when they were young. And we haven't any way of knowing whether they ever spent ten minutes in conversation all the time they were in this house together. Chances are," finished Burke, "that they were perfect strangers to each other. After all, do you know every man and every woman who came within twenty miles of you the year you were twenty-five, Riley?"

"I'm twenty-two," Riley admitted, a little crestfallen.

"What are the names of the Basque and the German lad on the top floor, and what are the names and nationalities of those three boys who were hovering around Dulcy that first night?" asked Burke purposefully.

Riley wilted. "You win. I don't know. If I ever heard their names mentioned, except at the inquests, I'd never heard them enough to remember. O.K., Cahoots didn't know Terracci and Lizzie. Then who killed 'em? Here we are back again."

"I'm supposed to be a policeman, not a fortuneteller," Burke said. "I've been making connections between these people till I feel like a telephone operator, but I can't get anywhere. I'll eat my badge if there's anything usable in all the facts we've been able to gather about everybody in the house. I even know that Jane here had her tonsils out at the age of five, had an appendix operation and a broken ankle in high school years and was engaged to two home town boys at the same time, but I can't seem to draw any conclusions, somehow. All the rest of my findings are just that unconnected."

A long-distance telephone call to the Chief of Police back in my town had probably given him all the material he'd come out with so casually, but somehow it made me feel as if somebody had torn aside a curtain so that everybody could look upon my private life. I have since realized that you can't very well get police to discover murderers without giving them a chance at the private lives of people who might be innocent of any crime or complicity, but it didn't strike me then.

And by the time I had stopped feeling unmasked, we were so deep in the next episode that I couldn't come up for air.

It all happened because of a jar of my orange marmalade.

16

We were ready to eat again. I wondered what Riley and Burke had done about meals before they got into the habit of poking their heads into my room to see if there was food forthcoming.

The steak and salad end of the budget had pretty well petered out before the afternoon when Burke and Riley got hungry right around teatime. Not that we ever had tea. Policemen and reporters seem to have laws against tea. Coffee was what they wanted, when nothing stronger was available, and like most men, they had a sweet tooth. Strangely, they didn't seem at all bothered by the possibilities of poisoning in my food, in spite of what had happened to Kay Johnson.

I had said something the day before about orange marmalade, and when they sat down and found that the little yeast rolls I'd made were without marmalade, they were as disappointed as Butch had been when he had to sell his bicycle to pay tuition.

Burke said casually: "There's a lot of stuff in jars in that cubbyhole of yours in the cellar. I guess maybe there wouldn't be any marmalade there?" It was a question, and I answered it:

"There's some there if you'll go down with me to get it. I'm not going into any cellars with murder in the house.

I've thought all along that you didn't pay enough attention to cellars, you policemen. There's plenty in cellars
besides jam and mice."

Burke said: "Ahoy, jam. Let's go." He armed himself
with my pancake turner and turned up his collar as if going out in the wintry blast. That was his idea of humor.

We were at the bottom of the narrow stairs when I
heard the sound of the click again.

"There's that mouse-trap again," I told Burke. "I haven't
thought of it since that first time you came down with me
to get jam. Sounds like a glass breaking, almost, or like
somebody trying to attract our attention."

Burke grabbed my arm so suddenly I almost stumbled
down the whole flight of stairs. "What's that?" he asked
sharply. "What click?"

I listened again, but couldn't hear anything this time.
"Just a mouse trap, I guess. There must be mice in a house
this old. I told you I heard one that other day—remember?"

"But you didn't tell me—" Burke wasn't casual now.
"And, Miss Jane—there isn't a mousetrap in the whole
cellar. Mrs. Meyer says that there haven't been any for
months. She used some kind of red squill and cleared them
all out, the rats and mice, I mean. She doesn't need traps.
What was that click like and where did it come from?"

I listened again, but couldn't hear anything unusual. A
couple of belated flies droned in the slow drunken manner
of chilly cellar weather. There was coal dust in the musty
air. I shivered a little, feeling that I should have worn my
coat.

"There. That's it," announced Burke, and I nodded, as
I caught the faint click that was so much like the crackle
of broken glass or the snap of a mouse trap.

Burke grabbed at my arm. "Go back upstairs and wait
for me in your room. Save me some coffee. Send Riley
down here so he doesn't eat everything himself before I

get up. It's probably a cricket or a mouse in the walls, but we'll investigate anyhow."

He didn't have to tell me twice. I was up in my room and was telling Riley about it before another two minutes were past.

I washed my dusty hands and sat back in my chair to figure things out while I waited for the men . . .

The next thing I knew I was waking up because Riley was shaking at my arm with hands that were black with coal.

His face was streaked with black until it looked like something made up for a minstrel show, and through the soot there was a tone of sickish green. Riley had seen things that were not nice to see.

"Jane," he ordered, and bless me if I didn't accept his orders as meekly as a wife, "wake up and fix us some coffee. We need it, both of us. Warm it while we wash up. Burke's got to go to headquarters in a minute, but he needs a cup of coffee, unless—I don't suppose that you'd have a bottle of whiskey?"

I was still half asleep, and I simply couldn't make myself understand what he was talking about. "Whiskey— why whiskey? Of course I haven't any whiskey."

"He needs it and so do I. Even a policeman, who gets used to seeing things, has a few limits."

He didn't go into any further details, except to say: "Go ahead. Get that coffee finished and on the table, there's a good girl, and we'll wash up and get time for a cup while we wait for the coroner and the rest of the homicide men."

He was gone before I could ask any more questions, and I realized that there must be another murder and that the best thing I could do was to obey orders and get hot coffee on the table, without orange marmalade.

When he and Burke came in, both were clean and neat, like good little boys who have eaten too much and been sick and are ready to do anything they are told for a while. Even Burke's hands were shaking when I poured out the hot coffee and gave it to him. He turned away from the hot rolls and didn't even look at the jelly I'd put out as a substitute for the marmalade.

"What do you know about George?" he asked finally, after the second cup of coffee.

"Nothing. I know that he roomed with Broad and Henry. He worked in the drugstore with Henry, I think. Is it George? Is he dead?"

Burke nodded. "Deader than—than anybody else in the case. He's been dead for a long time—ever since the first murders, maybe longer. It's possible that he died even before Miss Lizzie. God knows he looks like it."

He turned a little paler, if possible, and put down his cup with a shudder of distaste that the coffee didn't really deserve.

"Was that the doorbell? They ought to be here in a minute. Listen, Miss Jane, did Henry and George fight about Dulcy?"

"I don't know. I never heard them fighting. I never heard either of them fighting at all, except the day that I heard Dulcy and Henry, and then I couldn't hear what they said. Maybe they weren't fighting, but their voices did sound like it. For all I know, they may have been talking about the weather."

"You couldn't hear a word, Miss Jane?" Burke insisted.

"Not a word except—" I remembered—"I thought, after Henry left, that I heard Dulcy say: 'Milton'. But there isn't any Milton here in the house. Maybe it was a pet name she had for Henry, although I don't see how you'd get Milton from Henry. There's the doorbell, Mr. Burke."

He and Riley both left when the coroner and the rest of the men from the homicide bureau came. By this time the sight of their little bags and their cameras didn't seem

so odd to me, but I went back into my room and closed
the door, by Burke's order, and began to think that if these
murders kept up much longer I'd be taking up fancy work
to pass the hours that I had to spend secluded in my room.

Burke wouldn't let me leave the house except when
he or another policeman was with me. And there simply
wasn't anything to do in my room except cook and clean,
and you can't be a housewife all the time, especially if you
are having a vast curiosity about what's going on in the
rest of the house.

Riley came and went, and so did Cahoots and the mailman. Probably Mrs. Meyer did, but I hadn't seen her recently to be sure. And Betty and Torry were somewhere
away from the house. I hadn't seen Bill Broad except a
couple of times since he had stopped being an invalid, so
when the knock at the door proclaimed his presence, I was
entirely willing to let him come in and drape his long lean
figure across the arm of my lounging chair. If Bill Broad
posed, at least he did it becomingly.

He still looked a little pale after his escape from death.

"What's all the activity?" he demanded. "And while
you're telling me, Jane, you might pour me a cup of coffee. I like it almost cold, and with no sugar and not much
cream."

I fixed it for him, and he relaxed into the chair by
swinging his long elegant legs over the arm, and then sat
as comfortably as a Duke in a Mayfair novel, listening to
what I told him.

He didn't seem to be too much disturbed. "I'm not exactly shocked," he put it, "because I've suspected since the
night of his disappearance that George was dead, unless he
was the murderer himself. And since I had my little murdering trouble myself, I've been certain that George wasn't
the murderer, because he'd never strike at me. He wouldn't
have any reason to. George and I have always been friendly,

but not intimate enough for high emotion, if you get what I mean."

I thought I did, and said so. Of course Bill hadn't seen George the way Riley and Burke had, and that's the reason he wasn't so upset. Yet his reason for not believing George the murderer struck me as interesting.

"Tell me about George, Bill. Where did he come from? What did he do? What was he like?"

"A rather nondescript young fellow, I thought. Nice enough, but not very interesting. He and Henry were fond of Dulcy. But Henry really loved her. George thought he did."

I thought of another bone I had to pick with Bill. "Listen, Bill," I began, "why did you tell Riley that Henry said such complimentary things about me when they weren't true? It was Dulcy he was in love with, and you suggested that it might be me."

Bill, to my amazement, laughed. "I had to get a rise out of you some way. I've been trying to make a date with you ever since you've been in this house. You wouldn't pay any attention to me when I was decent to you, so I thought I'd be unjust to you and see if resentment could build up a little interest. I was too upset that night to get the idea straight, but it was something like that."

"I see," I returned, but I didn't, not really.

"There's another thing," Bill started again, putting down his cup and taking one of the yeast rolls I'd made for Burke and Riley. "I lied to you that night, to you and to Riley. Because I half thought that you and Riley had murdered Henry and Miss Lizzie and I thought I'd give you a break."

This startled me so that I sat straight up. "What do you mean?"

"I mean that I didn't call the police when I pretended to. I even cut the wire later on, to throw the phone out of wack so nobody else would phone before you got away." Broad was sitting there as quietly as if he hadn't thrown a bomb at me.

"You—cut the wire," I repeated stupidly, remembering the shiny thing in Riley's hand.

"Yes. I cut the wire. I'll confess to the cop, some day, if I get a chance. I owe him something for saving my life. I cut the wire. And all for you and Riley, Jane, and I didn't get a smile, let alone a thank you."

"Then what was Riley doing with—" I stopped, realizing that I didn't know what Riley had had in his hand.

"He wasn't cutting it, although I heard somebody say that he'd been seen cutting the cord. As a matter of fact, I think that he was probably trying to fix it in the place I cut." Bill Broad took a bite of my roll and added some jelly.

"Then why did he admit having cut it?" I asked, completely bewildered.

"Because he thinks that you cut it. That's evident. Or else—listen, Jane, are you absolutely sure about Riley? I keep thinking and thinking where I could have taken that poison. And the thing that goes around and around in my mind is the fact that Riley gave me an aspirin and something to drink after it, just before I went to sleep. Did he tell you?"

"No. He didn't tell me. But an aspirin—that couldn't be—" Desperately I tried to hold on to the remnants of my sanity. This was terrible. Yet it was no more than I had often suspected of Riley, myself.

"No. The aspirin mightn't have been poison. But there was something he gave me afterwards, to make the aspirin work more quickly on my headache, he said." Bill Broad reached for another roll and added grimly: "It almost stopped my headache permanently, at that."

"But surely there is—somebody else." I couldn't believe him. Not Riley. Anybody but Riley. Yet there were so many

things about him I hadn't understood. And even Burke had
wondered, in spite of himself, about Riley.

"Isn't there anybody else who could have given it to
you?"

"Nobody else. The mailman gave me a headache powder
earlier in the day, but that didn't have any ill effects at all,
I'm sure," he said, and I was overtaken again by hope.

"But the mailman is a suspect—maybe the medicine
worked later. Maybe that was what made you sick. Maybe
the mailman is the murderer." I was eager for any excuse
to change his opinion.

"I don't see how. That was an hour earlier. I had this
headache," he explained, "and I was on my way upstairs
when the mailman met me. He was on his way down. He
asked what was wrong with me, and I told him about this
headache, and he went up to his room and got this powder
and gave it to me and told me to take it and some drops
he gave me in the water afterwards. I did, but it didn't
help any. I even felt a little sick, nauseated, as if I'd eaten
something that disagreed with me, because the headache
kept getting worse and worse. Then Riley came along, and
went to his room for the stuff he gave me and stood over
me while I took it, and that's all I remember," he finished
simply.

"You seem to take it very easily," I said, almost with
resentment. Here was a man who was matter of fact about
a murder attempt that had almost taken his life.

"After all, why not? I can imagine murdering somebody
if I thought it was the only way to get what I want," he said,
helping himself to another roll. I wondered if Burke would
still be hungry enough to want food after his long session
in the cellar and whether I'd better keep some for him.

"But it wasn't pleasant for you—or for the rest of them."
I reminded him. I saw him shudder, and he put down the
last roll very quickly.

"If I meet the man who made me feel that way," he said, "I'll have a very nice time with his front teeth meeting my fist."

And just at that minute, the door opened and in came Burke and Riley.

17

I wasn't sure why the coming of these men should have made me think suddenly of Dulcy. Yes, I was, too. Because she had come in exactly that quick way while I had been talking to my brothers. But the men had come in the door while Dulcy had appeared on the balcony. It seemed suddenly very important that I tell Burke about this somehow.

Burke and Riley both frowned at the idea of Broad lounging there, consuming rolls and coffee, but after all, they did the same thing often enough themselves. When I looked at Riley's audacious eyes and crest of red hair I couldn't believe in Broad's suspicion of him. Yet the two young men distrusted each other. You could just see them bristling, like two strange dogs meeting for the first time.

Burke didn't say anything. He just kept watching the two of them as if their actions would tell him something he'd been wanting to know for a long time. Not for the first time I wondered just how far Burke trusted Riley. I was even a little suspicious at the amount of time he spent with him. Because that might be in order to keep an eye on him for police purposes.

I edged toward Burke and managed to say, under my breath: "I want to talk to you a minute, privately."

Burke, without answering, said: "Riley, I want you and Broad to do a job for me. Go along to headquarters with the men, and after they get there, wait until word comes from the morgue. Tell Thompson I'll phone him about further plans. Riley, you can phone your office from head-quarters if you want to."

"Why me?" Broad asked lazily. I wondered whether he wasn't just a little frightened at the idea of going off with a man who had, according to his own suspicions, almost murdered him.

"Because I'll need you to give us further information about George. You were one of his roommates, and the other one is dead and therefore can't be called on for information."

"Not very well unless you've a Ouija board," agreed Broad, getting up languidly, and brushing his hands free of crumbs.

"Better speed it up and you can ride down to head-quarters with Curly. Better get your overcoats. It's turning cold."

They went out, and it didn't seem to be much more than five minutes before they came downstairs again and I heard them go out the front door and down the steps to where Curly waited for them in the little police depart-ment car. The rest of the men had gone off by that time, taking all their pictures and measurements. I had no way of telling how long everything had taken, since I had fall-en asleep waiting.

Burke went to the phone, and although I couldn't hear the actual words he spoke into the mouthpiece, I knew that he was giving careful orders to somebody at police head-quarters. Then he gave some more orders to a uniformed cop who remained in the hall. This man went clumping upstairs, and Burke and I were left alone. He closed the door behind him and went back to the big chair, where he slumped, looking too dispirited for words.

"Mr. Burke, how could anybody get onto my balcony, except from this room?" I asked, and was startled to see how Burke sat up immediately.

"Who did?" he barked. "Are you sure?"

"Yes. Dulcy did. Remember when my brothers were here? Well, I had just told them that I had no intention of giving money to Dulcy for her beauty shop, and then I looked up and there she was outside my window, on the balcony. By the time I got there, she was gone. And I know that she didn't get into this room at all. She got to the balcony somewhere from the outside."

"And if she got there from the outside," added Burke, "then there isn't any reason why Torry shouldn't have gotten there from the outside that first night."

"Then he hadn't been in my room at all?" I was eager, and then I remembered the bloodstains. Where had they come from? And the bloodstained coins, and the blood-stain on my bathrobe, and the dime in my pocket?

"Your guess is as good as mine. Look, Miss Jane. Do you know what this is?" He took from his pocket a flaky pink bit of something. I simply couldn't make up my mind what it was. Not pink wallpaper cleaner, although it looked something like that. Not a piece of papier-mâché from a broken doll head, although it looked a little like that, too.

I told him about these two "almosts," and he said: "You may have something there. Could you think of anything else at all?"

"The only other thing I can remember is a box I made when I was a kid. I took a cigar box and then pasted wet paper around it until it dried and then painted it blue, and slipped the cigar box out from under so I had a sort of home-made composition stuff for my box."

Burke was excited. I could see that. "Say it over again," he said. "You used something for a mold and made something

out of wet papers that held the mold of the box under-
neath. Then you painted it blue and it looked like this,
except for the color?"

"Exactly. Mine wasn't so smooth and flaky as that when
it got broken, but that's probably because I didn't put the
paste on the flakes of paper right. Or maybe my shellac
was too sticky when I finished the box."

"Let me get this straight: The bits of paper get pasted
to the foundation box?"

"No—o. Not exactly. You grease the box so the paper
will come off in a solid piece later. I broke my box taking it out, but some of the smarter ones got it out whole.
Some of them used blocks of modeling clay or plaster to
build their boxes on."

Burke was insistent. "You took bits of paper, soaked
them in paste, put them on your mold. Then you painted
your box, and shellacked it after it was finished. O.K.?"

"O.K." I agreed, wondering what in the world all of
this had to do with the murders.

Burke pondered aloud: "And I suppose that you don't
know whether there's any such thing as a sort of false face
made in this same way."

"Yes." All of this seemed like such a long time ago.
"There was a school play we went to, once. We made up
as one another. I made a mask like my teacher's face, and
everybody said that I looked just like her, except for height
and figure, that is," I announced proudly, and sat back to
wonder why Burke's face was suddenly relaxing into the
first hint of serenity I'd seen on it for a long time. His
voice was as casual as I'd ever heard it when he said:

"Have you ever mentioned this trick of making boxes
and masks to anybody in this house? And, Miss Jane, have
you ever seen anybody in the house making a mask? Or
have you seen a mask made by anybody here?"

With sudden terror I remembered: "I told everybody. The first time I had a party here, when I was lonesome and invited everybody in the house in for cookies and coffee, I was bringing out every funny story I ever had to break the ice, and I told one about something that happened when I put on my teacher's mask and fooled the class. But that only happened because the lights went out one evening when we were having a class meeting. I put a scarf around the edges of my hair and stood alongside a chair so they thought it was the teacher sitting down, and it was really me standing up."

"In a dim light, almost no light at all? You mentioned that?"

"In a dim light. Not much more light than we had here when the lights went out and the candles were lighted."

Burke changed the subject. "Is there any way to get to your balcony from the street?"

"Not that I know of. I guess that you could use a ladder from downstairs in the basement flat. There's a little area way down there, under the balcony. Somebody could climb up."

"That's Mrs. Meyer's flat down there, isn't it? Are she and Dulcy on good terms?" asked Burke.

I thought hard. "I can't remember ever hearing them talking together, before the murders, except when Dulcy paid her rent, I guess." I was staring, not at Burke, but at the deserted table, wondering whether I ought to get up and clear off the cups, the crumbs and all the rolls and jam.

"And if a ladder could come from downstairs, maybe one could come from upstairs. Isn't there a balcony above this?" Burke got up and went to the window. He opened it so that the heavy breeze chilled the room and made the tablecloth flap. He stuck out his head and looked up to see the balcony overhead.

I followed him and looked up, too. "There's a fire-escape from the third floor balcony to the second," I offered, "but not from the second floor to the first."

"Why not?" snapped Burke, as if I knew.

"It was probably taken off. We have two flights of stairs between the first floor and the second. I always had an idea that there was some sort of a folding ladder from the upstairs balcony down to this one, but I don't see it now."

"But there was one?" asked Burke sharply.

"I think so. I'm not sure. I haven't seen it recently enough to be sure. But don't they have to have a ladder, for the fire laws here?"

"Come along with me. No. Wait," snapped Burke. He disappeared and closed the door behind him and I could hear his footsteps going up the stairs.

Then, above me, as I stood at the window, I saw his figure on the second-floor balcony. "Are you there, Miss Jane?" he called.

"Yes. Do you see anything?"

"I see almost everything," Burke answered. Swinging from the grooved iron floor of the upstairs balcony came an iron ladder. "Look out down there, Miss Jane," called Burke, and he started down the ladder. As soon as he was safely down he closed the window and came into my room. But as I watched from behind the glass I saw the iron ladder go swinging back up to its position under the floor of the upper balcony. As I saw the flash of the black ladder I realized that I had seen exactly the same thing on the day that I had seen Dulcy there on the balcony.

I said so to Burke, and he nodded grimly. "Have you seen this at any other time," he asked, "besides when you saw Dulcy?"

"No. Not that I can remember, except the first month I was here when we had the fire scare."

"When was that?"

"Oh, just after I came here—the day after my party, by the way. Broad must have fallen asleep with a lighted cigarette or something. I'd almost forgotten. There was no damage except that Broad had to buy new pajamas and a pair of pillow cases, and we all lost an hour of sleep in the early morning."

"The ladder wasn't there the day we examined the upstairs balcony, the day after Terracci's murder. It must be detachable."

"They sometimes are. I remember hearing somebody mention that the woman who had this apartment before me kept pots of flowers out on this balcony. Maybe she wanted the ladder taken off so it wouldn't break her plants if it fell accidentally."

Burke looked disgusted: "And we have fire laws in this town," he said disgustedly. "But maybe the inspector was a sucker for pretty women and she was pretty."

"Dulcy said once that she looked like a horse. And few men," I said carefully, "like the equine type of beauty."

"At some time, then, just before the murder of Madame Terracci the ladder was taken off. It was probably there at the time when Torry was put on the balcony, and we know it was there when Dulcy went on this balcony for reasons of her own."

"But aren't these things very heavy? Are you sure that the ladder wasn't just hidden under the floor of the upper balcony. Maybe the men didn't look carefully."

"If they didn't, I'll break their necks cheerfully," Burke promised, not at all cheerful himself. "So now we don't really know whether it was ever taken away, and I'm as much a fool as any of them for not realizing that this was part of a fire-escape system. That should be just part of the routine." He glared at me angrily, as if it was all my fault, which it certainly wasn't.

We had another stack of unrelated facts, but by now Burke seemed to be much more excited about these than about the others.

The murder victims were:
    Henry
    Miss Lizzie
    Madame Terracci
    Kay Johnson
    George.

The attacks that were murderous but had not ended in death had been on:
    Bill Broad
    Torry.

This left a minimum number of those in the house who were not victims and among whom therefore it was likely that the murderer would be found:
    Mrs. Meyer
    Riley
    Cahoots Smith
    The mailman with the odd name of Peregrine Rogers
    Dulcy
    Betty
    Jane

I put my own name down there because, although I knew that of course I was innocent, it was likely that somebody still suspected me.

Betty was undoubtedly as innocent as poor Torry.

That left three men and two women in whose ranks the murderer would undoubtedly be found. I didn't know then why we so completely ruled out the men on the top floor. After all, there were five of them. But I discovered later that Burke had kept a constant guard so that none of them had come into the rest of the house except through the halls, and that every one had been in sight every minute he had been in the halls.

The fire-escape had been covered, too, with additional guards. With so many policemen busy at our house, I wondered what would have happened if there had been many other murders in town, but maybe we were more important than I realized.

So there they were, five murder suspects.

And five murder victims, besides.

18

At the inquest on George it was reported that he had been dead for some time. It was almost impossible, from the condition of the body, as the coroner's physician put it delicately, to tell exactly when the death had occurred. Yet the chances were that he had died first, even before Miss Lizzie and Henry. It was at this inquest, too, that we found where the poisons, the whole bunch of them, had come from.

When Henry's brother had come to take Henry's body back home, the police got from him a statement that Henry had always been interested in poisons and their antidotes, that indeed he had once written a university paper on the subject, and that Henry's brother suspected that Henry himself may have had enough poison in his possession, as the brother put it, "to poison the whole houseful, let alone those few, but Henry didn't do it, because Henry killed himself. He was always threatening to, anyhow."

Well, Burke was equally certain that Henry had not committed suicide. Yet the origin of the poisons was clear too. If these had been in his possession, who would be likely to know it?

His roommates, George and Bill. But George was dead, and Bill denied absolutely having seen anything of any poisons.

His sweetheart, Dulcy. But Dulcy said that she wouldn't know a poison from a hole in the ground. Dulcy also denied having had an ulterior purpose in being on my balcony. She says that she saw me with a couple of good-looking young men and wanted to find out who they were. The ladder had been down at the time she used it.

No, she had never used the ladder or the balcony before, and had no memory of ever having noticed it except at the time of the fire.

Nobody else knew anything about the ladder.

And nobody at all knew anything about the body of George.

Except for the clicks made by some rats materialized from somewhere trying to get at the body which had been locked in a sort of glass-fronted cupboard in a wine bin in the cellar, George might not have been discovered for some time. Judging from the tooth marks of the rats on the wooden parts of the cupboard, according to Burke's testimony, the rats might have been trying to get at it for some time. I had undoubtedly heard them at least twice.

The policemen who had searched the cellar had to explain why they hadn't gone into the wine cellar beyond the coal hole, and they were vehement in explaining that they didn't know that there was a wine cellar and thought that the coal bins extended all the way to the back of the house.

There was no way of determining whether the body had been carried down cellar after death or whether George had been lured down with some fantastic story and had been killed right there where his temporary coffin was prepared for him. About that time my nausea prevented me from getting a very clear picture of some of the rest of the details, but I did revive enough to hear that the poison was the same as the one that had killed Henry, but that no signs of chocolate had been found.

There had been, so far as anybody could tell, no sign of blood on the body that could have accounted for the bloodstains in my room and the splash of blood on my mantelpiece.

Nothing was said at the inquest about the matter of the mask. By this time it was beginning to filter through even my stupid head that Henry's appearance as a ghost had probably been caused by one of the other men coming in with a sort of mask copying Henry's face. I could tell that that is what had excited Burke, but I still couldn't see why the murderer, if it was the murderer, should have found it necessary to go to such childish extremes to produce fear in an already horrible situation.

I went to George's funeral because Bill Broad asked me to, and said that there wasn't anybody to go except us, in the house. George didn't have any family at all. The funeral was at an undertaking parlor, and the body was sealed in one of those metal coffins. You never saw such a morbid crowd as the one that followed us to the cemetery. Bill Broad had bought a cemetery lot for George. "Poor devil—there's nobody else to do it for him," he said. "Maybe somebody'll be doing the same for me pretty soon."

I supposed he was referring to his own recent escape from a death that might still seize him. Dulcy didn't go to the funeral at all, but she went around looking like a lost soul, and far more frightened than she had seemed after Henry's death or Kay Johnson's.

Her very hair looked a tone less bright, which was probably, I thought sagely, because she hadn't had time to get it touched up again, what with all the murders.

For the first time I heard somebody mention the finding of a bottle of chloroform with Henry's fingerprints on it. Of all places, it had been beside George's body. Yet the only time during the whole period when chloroform had been in question was when we had found Miss Lizzie.

Then the smell of chloroform had been almost as strong as the smell of garlic that they said was the phosphorus poison.

Nobody had yet discovered, so far as I knew, why the stage had been set for a breakfast for two in Madame Terracci's room, or why there was blood in my room. They had found, by this time, that the blood was of the same rare type as Torry's blood, but that didn't help any, because nobody could possibly have hit Torry in my room while I was sleeping.

Burke was at the door so early the next morning that I had to slip into a clean starched housedress and run out to open the hall door for him with my face still shiny from a soap and water scrubbing and with my hair combed back from my face in the neat but not beautiful style that is known as the bathtub knot. Since I let my hair grow, it's convenient to be able to pin it back now and then just for tidiness' sake.

He looked approvingly at me when I snapped: "Why don't you get a key? So long as you're here, you might as well come in to breakfast, though what my reputation is worth after all this I don't know."

"Your life will be worth something, though," he said casually, coming in and closing the door behind him.

While I rattled around the pots and pans, he startled me by carefully making up the couch that was my bed and picking up around the room, in a housewifely fashion that didn't go with his occupation. He'll make a neat husband for some woman some day, I thought, although for my part I'll take one not quite so orderly by nature.

I made French toast, and Burke squeezed orange juice for both of us. The coffee was strong, and I had cream for a change, since it was too early in the morning for the policemen and reporters to have come in searching for food and drinking up the cream for my coffee and even the canned milk. And I do hate coffee black.

After he had finished his breakfast, he sat there for a minute while I began to clear the table. "It hasn't been long, Miss Jane," he said, "but it's been hectic. Outside of one of these literary murders or a gangster job, this is the biggest number of murders I've ever seen in one house. You don't know who it was who did the murders, do you?"

"I haven't any real idea. I've narrowed it down in my mind to three men and two women." I remembered my list and got out the paper on which I had scrawled down the names and gave it to him.

He studied them carefully. "My list is narrower than yours, and the names aren't exactly the same. I won't say much more now, but I'm beginning to have a hunch, little girl. And for that reason I want you to promise me something: Don't be so free with guests. Don't let the folks in the house come in here and lounge around eating this way, and don't go out unless you have to. When you do have to go, let me know, through the guard outside your door. Phone all orders to the store and get your sunshine out on your little balcony, being sure that the ladder is safely up before you do."

Half resentfully I put in: "You seem to be sure that somebody's out to get my scalp."

"I'm sure," he said, "that somebody is out to kill you and until we are absolutely sure who it is, the only safe thing for you is to make a hermitage out of this room."

I wasn't sure that this was the right word, but obviously he was very sincere. "Is that anything like a monastery?" I asked, trying to be funny.

"It's the wrong sex," he said casually, and then insisted: "But, Miss Jane, this means living or dying for you, you know, and you'll be dead a long time, so you'd better postpone it for a while if you can." He left then, but came back within fifteen minutes to take up the conversation again.

"But how can I keep 'em out—the people in the house?" I asked.

"Very simply. Have you ever had the smallpox?"

"I was vaccinated against it when I was three," I answered witheringly.

"You are suspected of having the smallpox now. And since the hospitals are overcrowded and aren't any too keen about contagious diseases, and since the pesthouse is overcrowded with scarlet fever, you are staying at home until we are certain that it is smallpox. But you are in quarantine."

"It sounds fishy." I was dubious.

"It won't, when I get through with you." He began to take out of his pocket a little bag. Unfolded, it divulged a couple of stickers labeled: "Smallpox Quarantine" in big red letters.

"These are forged," he advised shamelessly. "Besides, if you really had smallpox, they'd have you out of this house so quick it would make your head swim. But maybe we can get away with it. Roll up your sleeves and come a little closer."

In a businesslike fashion he was opening a small paintbox and revealing neat brushes and colors. "I haven't had so much fun since the day we painted my brother so the family thought he had the measles. The idea is to make splotches like a good strong smallpox. The lights won't be bright. You won't be close enough for anybody to see you clearly, and even I will have to see you on the sly."

"Rendezvous at midnight," I commented bitterly. "And do I stay here for the rest of my life?"

"If you want any more life," he said so solemnly that it frightened me, and I shut up and let him paint my face and arms with some ghastly sores that were almost real. Then he lowered the shades, pasted the stickers on the door, and said: "Better not wash your face and hands until I'm around to help you to get some more smallpoxes."

I couldn't help a small giggle when I saw my face in the dim mirror. The pulled-down shades helped the illusion, too, so that I looked like something escaped from a contagious hospital sure enough. Suddenly this all seemed terribly convincing, and I stopped thinking how funny and silly it was.

"But would a murderer be scared off by a smallpox sign?" I asked.

"By a smallpox sign, locked doors and a police guard—especially if several of the people in the house, including the murderer, are allowed a peep at you through the window to see those realistic sores. They're the neatest I've ever made. Doc gave me lessons. He's coming in a minute to check up and see if you're beautiful enough for realism."

The doctor came just about then, and made a few adjustments of the neatly painted sores. He brought with him a hatchet-faced woman a foot taller than I was, and some seventy pounds heavier. She was in nurse's uniform, but had none of a nurse's kindly expression—that is, the expression that nurses are all supposed to have.

"Ma Taylor will take care of you," Burke said. "She'll take in the grocery orders, or even meals from the restaurant at the corner if we can manage that."

"No. Can't I even cook?" I begged. "I'll die of boredom."

"Sleep in the daytime," Burke advised, "and do your cooking at night. Then sometimes I can sneak in to see you. These preparations aren't normal ones for smallpox, but they'll do for the present. I thought of advising you to go to a hotel, but here I can keep you under my eyes."

"Any murderer who can get past Ma Taylor," put in the nurse grimly, "is good."

"This murderer is one of the best," warned Burke, and he and Doc tiptoed out of the place while the nurse got me undressed and into the remade bed and sat herself beside me with a magazine, although I noticed that she closed her eyes and didn't even try to read. But before she settled down she locked the door and the windows carefully, and I wondered whether the books were right when they said that the ventilation from these old-fashioned grates was as good as an open window.

I'm a talkative soul, and Ma Taylor wouldn't talk. Except for a shrewd and very cynical comment now and then, she was as wordless as a dictionary cover with all the pages torn out.

I have seldom if ever been so bored as I was during the next three days. I remained in bed with the police nurse guarding me but not talking to me. I had a big enough dose of silence to last me for the rest of my life. I hadn't had a private bath since I'd been in the place, but now we had one, from necessity. There was a locked door between my room and the first-floor bathroom, but I'd always gone through the hall door, since the other room on the same floor used the same bath. But now the bathroom was unlocked and turned over to our use, with the halldoor locked instead. With this we had one of what a friend of mine had once called 'self-contained flats'. She was an English girl, so maybe that's what they call 'em in her home town.

But I was bored. I slept enough during the daytime to make me stay away from sleep for a month after all this was over. I didn't know what was happening outside the door.

Burke or Curly personally supervised the leaving of food supplies in front of our door, and Ma Taylor took them in and started out to do the cooking. I have seldom had worse coffee and never had worse food. Why, that woman could take a two-inch steak, well hung, and with all the right accompaniments, and could turn out a piece of fried chamois skin. Finally I put my foot down, literally.

"Listen, Ma Taylor," I said firmly. "I'll lie here and sleep all day. Then at night you lie here with the shades drawn and let me do the cooking. Anybody who looks in can see you lying on the bed and will think that I'm you working at the stove behind that screen."

So that was how we did it. And Ma Taylor got half good natured, although never quite voluble, when she tasted my pot roast with carrots and potatoes. Some day, I thought, I'd teach that woman to cook, but I had to acknowledge regretfully that it couldn't be done. Before I met her I'd thought that everybody could cook. Now I know better.

One day several people gathered on the balcony outside my window. Burke was among them. So was Riley. Broad was there, too, and Smith, and the mailman. Then the rest of the bunch took their turn and all of them looked sad and regretfully at me through the glass while I lay motionless on the bed, looking at them from under my eyelids. I didn't dare to giggle, and I wanted to, somehow.

They were all satisfied, then, about my sickness. Dulcy seemed to find a bit of shuddering satisfaction at the sight of my sores, such of them as she could see by peering through the glass and the curtain.

Now that I look back on it, I find it incredible that I could have gotten away with the game for even as long as I did. Riley and Broad sent in flowers and fruit that Ma Taylor handled with gloves on and wouldn't let me touch— not even the most beautiful peaches that ever grew, and grapes as big as small plums. It seemed like a terrible waste when she got Burke to have them taken away without letting me taste one. And she wouldn't let the flowers stay in the room, even, for some silly reason.

I didn't squabble about it. She just laid down the law, and I was as meek about that as she was about my cooking.

And that's the way we got on till the night, just about two, when I heard the noise on the balcony.

19

There was very little light in the room, and what little there was lay on the floor. Ma Taylor had put a small lighted electric light bulb under the bed, of all places, so she could see where she was going in case she walked around, and still not have a light in the "patient's" eyes.

The patient was particularly well fed, at the moment. Around midnight we had supped on omelets with mushrooms, a vegetable salad and coffee, and after a rather private meal behind the screen, I was ready to get back in bed and play sick as long as anybody wanted me too. I was even ready to drowse a little.

The room was so quiet that I could hear the traffic on the nearest big street. Somewhere a church clock struck two, and I heard men's voices shouting a couple of blocks away. Then I heard the scrape of feet and a body striking against something. Then a murmur as if a man were swearing to himself when he barked his shin in the dark, and outside on my balcony a man stood, looking in.

I couldn't see who it was, except that he was tall. That meant that he might be Riley or Broad or Peregrine Rogers, the mailman. It wasn't Smith, and it wasn't Burke. That much I could see.

Ma Taylor was sitting beside my bed, and I noticed that she fingered something in her pocket. Could it be possible that this woman carried a gun to protect me?

This, then, was the moment for which we had prepared.

For the first time I wondered if perhaps Burke had not used me for bait. That was an idea. Because certainly a man intending murder wouldn't be scared off by a quarantine sign. In fact, the quarantine sign might be a welcome sight to a murderer, because it would keep other people away and give him a free hand with a girl weakened by sickness (so he thought, anyhow, probably). Of course there was the nurse, but how was the murderer to know that she was an iron guard armed with a gun?

And just at that moment a small knock came at the door leading to the hall.

There we were. On the balcony one person, at the door another.

The simplest thing was to do nothing at all. But Ma Taylor was a woman of action, and so am I. Every time I think of women who can get into bed and pull the covers over their heads when danger comes, I wonder anew at them. I'm not like that. I crave action. What I wanted more than anything else was to get up on my own feet and meet whatever was coming with my head high and my fist clenched. After all, I may be little, but I've got muscles. My brother taught me how to box, years ago, and I know just where to hit a man to do the most good, in the quickest amount of time.

I'd have to hit quickly if I hit at all, before a man got on his guard, because otherwise I'd be too little to have any real effect. But one blow could do the job if the man was off his guard, and Bud had trained me well.

If I hadn't seen that man on the balcony, watching the bed, I'd have gotten up when Ma Taylor hesitated and then walked toward the door, her hand on whatever was sagging her pocket.

I don't think that I ever felt so helpless and so frightened in my life, except perhaps the night of the first murders when I went downstairs in the dark, although maybe that wasn't quite so bad as this, because at least then I was on my own feet instead of lying in bed.

Ma Taylor, at the door, said sharply: "Who is it?"

Riley's voice: "I must see Jane. I just must see her. Let me in, Nurse."

"We're in quarantine. Smallpox. You know that."

"It's probably chickenpox," said Riley witheringly, "and even if it isn't, I was vaccinated last year again and it took. Let me in, Nurse. It's a matter of life or death."

Ma Taylor said firmly: "No. Tell me what you want to say and I'll see that the patient hears it when she wakes."

"The patient must get this information now. Wake her up or I will. And if I wake her in my own way I'll wake up the rest of the house too," warned Riley. I could hear every word, faintly but clearly through the heavy panels of the door.

This was like and yet unlike the experience when I had talked to Broad through the same door, on the night of the first murders.

"I can't wake my patient," insisted Ma Taylor stubbornly, knowing very well that I was wide awake. I know now that she thought this was the best way of getting the information Burke wanted, but I thought she was foolish then.

"I'm very good on war-whoops," Riley said. "The Indians couldn't do better, and my shrieks of 'Fire!' have started many a panic."

Ma Taylor hesitated. But she didn't open the door. "Give me the message. I'll wake her and give it to her," she agreed.

Riley said: "I've written it down. Here it is on this paper. Just give it to her, or read it to her if she isn't able to read it herself. She will be better if her mind is free from doubt. I'll sit here on the bottom step, and you can open the door or knock on your side of it when you are ready with her answer."

He slipped the paper under the door. I could see a white paper, much longer than ordinary copy sheets. It tore a little along the edges because it was a tight fit, but finally Ma Taylor picked it up.

The man on the balcony was crouching there, still looking in. He probably couldn't hear anything said in the room, or could he? I'd never tried to find out. Possibly he could hear faintly what Ma Taylor said and guess that somebody was talking to her out in the hall. And he could see the paper coming in under the door.

That much I knew. Now what would he do next? But it made me feel safer to know that Ma Taylor was back beside me. I don't know whether I felt safer to have Riley out in the hall where he could hear if we called. I didn't even know that it wasn't Riley of whom I should be scared.

But the crouching figure of that man on the balcony was what gave me cold feet. I could tell that Ma Taylor was acting out a part for his observation. She came close to the bed and leaned over me. "Wake up, Miss Jane," she said, gently touching me. I lay quiet for a minute and then stirred, trying to be as good an actress as Ma.

"What's the matter?" I whispered.

"Wake up. I want to talk to you. We have a message that I want you to read." Oddly, she didn't put on the lamp. Instead she took a flashlight from the table. Hers, it was. I had given to Butch the one that I had used that first night. She focused the light on the paper and propped me up with some pillows behind my back.

I could see that the man on the balcony was settling back on his haunches. He was probably keeping his eyes on the paper, but I knew that he wouldn't be able to see anything from that distance. I realized, too, that the reason why the lamp had not been put on was so that we shouldn't be in the spotlight and therefore helpless if the man should appear from the balcony. Also, so long as we were almost in the dark we could watch him as closely as he watched us. Of course we tried to appear unconcerned, because it was obvious that he didn't think he was observed at all, and so we put on an act as best we could.

The paper was a sheet of rough copy stuff about twice as long as the usual size, and it was typed on both sides.

I read the first paragraph through once without quite taking it in, and then began all over again, but Ma Taylor didn't read over my shoulder at all. She kept her eyes on the window and her hand on the gun in her big pocket.

Here is the letter. Burke gave it back to me, after the case was over. It is yellow and crumpled but still legible.

> "Dear Jane:
> "Somehow I can't feel that you are as sick as Burke makes out, or you would be in a hospital instead of at home. But Burke's got the right idea if he is using this scheme to keep you protected, except that I did hope that he'd trust me to see that no harm came to you. Well, it's necessary for me to tell you some things:
> "In the first place, don't let that mailman come within a foot of you. I don't trust that man. He spends every spare minute hovering around your door, and I've caught him on your balcony twice."

At this, I stopped reading and cast a look under my eyelashes at the man on the balcony. Yes, it might be Peregrine Rogers, the mailman. He was tall, in fact he was the only tall man on the suspect list, except Riley himself. Of course Broad was tall, but Broad wasn't a possible murderer, because he was one of the victims, and it was only because Burke and I had come at the right time that Broad wasn't dead with the rest of them.

But Riley could be guilty and could be casting suspicion on the mailman just to free himself of suspicion.

I went on with the letter:

> "I have found the answers to a lot of our questions. I've told Burke, but I want to tell you, because I feel that you should be warned. Listen, Jane, you are going to be the next victim if there is any possible way for the murderer to get to you. The main thing I want to tell you is to avoid opening any mail brought to you. Also, do not accept any packages from the hands of the mailman, even if your nurse takes them from Rogers and hands them to you. He'll find some way of getting to you if he can, and God knows what poison he'll try and how he'll get it to you."

The man on the balcony wasn't stirring. He was probably Rogers, I thought. I tried to see if one shoulder was higher than the other, as Rogers' was, from the mailbag, but I couldn't see. He was only a brooding crouching figure on the balcony.

I went back to the letter:

> "Jane, you must be careful. I send this to you at night to beg you to let me come in and see you. I'm not afraid of smallpox, if it's smallpox you have, and frankly I don't think it is. I've smelled smallpox, and this isn't it. It may be chickenpox, but I've had that, and I've been vaccinated against smallpox, so I'm not afraid of that, either. Besides, I won't be able to feel that you are entirely safe until I can sit in that room with you, beside your bed, with

my hand on my gun. And then you needn't be
afraid because I'll take care of you."

I could feel tears coming to my eyes. No, this boy was
never guilty. How could he be and write like that? I didn't
love him or anything romantic like that, but at that minute, I knew that he was a pretty swell boy and darned nice
to have for a friend.

"Here are the questions, and later come the
answers, although I won't tell you now how I
got the answers."

I stopped here to wipe my eyes on the handkerchief from
under my pillow, and I wondered how Ma Taylor could go
on without any human curiosity. I'd have grabbed the paper out of anybody's hand, myself. It was hard reading, all
of this typing in single space on both sides of the paper,
but it was probably the only way he could get the whole
thing on one piece of paper to slip it under the door.

"1. Why was the stage set for breakfast for two?
"2. Where did Burke find the little scrap of
    browned crisp pancake he showed us? You
    see, I've found out what it is now, though
    I didn't know then.
"3. Where did the bloodstains come from, in
    your room?
"4. Where did the bloodstained money come
    from, and the dime?
"5. Why was Miss Lizzie on her knees in an
    attitude of prayer, and how did her mur-
    derer get her to take the phosphorus?
"6. Were all the victims killed by the same
    murderer?

"7. Who made the masks? We found the one
     of Henry and we found one of you, but we
     don't know who made them.

"8. What connection was there between all
     the victims of the murderer? I have a very
     interesting answer to this question. I'll an-
     swer it later.

"9. Who sent the telegram that tried to accuse
     you of complicity in the murders?

"10. Who took the flavoring from your cup-
     board and added prussic acid to it before
     it was thrown from the upper balcony?
     This is what was done. I think that Burke
     knows it as well as I do. And your spunky
     stunt with the gingerbread was a brilliant
     piece of work, Jane.

"11. Who put your button under the box of
     candy in Terracci's room?

"12. Why didn't Broad have his coat on if
     he had been wandering around talking on
     that chilly night? This was a question you
     mentioned to me, Jane. Somehow I feel it's
     important.

"13. Where did Broad go when he slipped
     away while we were searching your room?

"There are some other questions, but these
     are the most striking right now. I want to
     tell you my answers for all of them, espe-
     cially the connection between the murders.
     Nobody has seemed to consider one direct
     possibility: Blackmail."

That bewildered me, so I stopped to think and to look
at the man on the balcony. Ma Taylor hadn't moved. Anybody would think, looking at her, that she was asleep. But
I knew that she wasn't, not Ma.

The man was standing again, and I saw that he was feeling to see if the window was locked. It was. Ma had seen to that.

I kept my hands on the letter, but my eyes were watching the man. I didn't dare take them away from him because I was terribly afraid.

I put the paper under the pillow and put out the light. "Ma," I said, in a whisper, "open the door and let Riley in. Then you call Burke. I'm getting up."

"You're doing no such thing," snapped Ma. "That's just what Burke wanted me to guard against."

"Then knock at the door and slip out a note asking Riley to get Burke on the phone and get him to send a policeman here right away."

"There are at least three policemen in the house," said Ma Taylor, "besides me, and I'm as much a policeman as they are."

She was plainly resentful, but she took the note I scribbled in the semi-dark, while I watched the man on the balcony with one eye, between words. And she knocked on the inside of the door and slipped out the note when she heard Riley's eager answer.

I had written: "There's a man on the balcony outside my room and I'm afraid. You may be right. It looks like the mailman. He's tall, anyhow. I haven't finished reading your letter, but I will." Then I added: "I'm glad that you aren't scared of smallpox."

Now remember that I had been thoroughly isolated all this time. Except that I had had flowers and fruit from Riley and Broad and therefore knew that they were still alive, I didn't know anything else about anybody in the house. More murders might have happened, for all I knew.

I heard Riley go to the phone, and I asked Ma Taylor to put out the light entirely so that the figure outside couldn't look in at all. I dressed quickly, and pinned back my hair which had been flowing on the pillow, sick room

fashion. I put on a jacket because it was cold in the room
after all the bedcovers had been piled on me, and I put on
shoes that didn't need lacing because I was afraid that my
numb fingers couldn't even have tied the knot.

It must have been about two-thirty in the morning by
this time.

I could hear Riley hang up the phone, and then I heard
the outer door close softly behind him.

I was afraid he was leaving the house till I realized that
he wanted to see the balcony from the outside. Then, in a
flash, everything happened at once. Instead of one figure
on the dark balcony there were four, tussling and fighting.
And then one figure brought something from his pocket
and crashed it down on another figure's head and then
three figures stood looking down at a fourth who lay in a
heap at their feet.

For the first time I saw that Ma Taylor had opened the
door to Burke, who must have been in the house all along,
and who now went to the window, opened it as casually
as if he had never put a quarantine sign on the door, and
flashed the beam of his electric torch on the face of the
crumpled figure.

Peregrine Rogers, the mailman. And he looked dead.
But Burke said: "There's a pulse. Better get him in here. I
saw all of that last business myself, every step of it."

"The case is closed. Let me get to the phone," burbled
Riley, who was on the balcony.

"Come into the room, Riley. Bring Rogers in. Curly,
phone for Doc. Ma, help me get him on the bed. All of you
stay here. And Ma, ask the policeman in the hall to whistle
for all the rest of the folks in the house to come down here
now. We're all ready. The case is cracked."

20

The marks of the pretended smallpox were still on my face, and it was hours before I thought to go and wash them off, because there were so many more things to be considered. Peregrine Rogers lay on my bed, his colorless face startling against the white of the pillow. And under that pillow were the answers to Riley's questions. I was to wait a long time before I ever saw those answers typed out in Riley's hunt-and-peck typing on the long copysheets.

Dulcy said, when she came in all curls and yesterday's make-up and feather-and-lace negligee: "Your smallpox seems to be doing well. Are those scars?"

"In a way," I said truthfully.

Burke turned over the patient to Doc and Ma Rogers, and the rest of us gathered in the far corner of the huge room. Somebody brought in chairs, and we sat around and waited. On the balcony Curly and another policeman were talking, and two others stood in the doorway, with several scattered at odd points in the room. I had never seen so many policemen gathered in one place before. And they weren't sleepy, either, the way that most of the other people there seemed to be.

Mrs. Meyer was sleepy but beautiful. Her shadowed eyes were glowing, her skin a dead-white velvet. She wore a trailing black velvet housecoat that needed only ermine to make it look queenly.

Broad and Riley and Rogers were all fully dressed in daytime clothes. So was Smith. I wondered whether everybody had gone to bed with clothes on. Or maybe they hadn't gone to bed at all.

Except for the fact that Rogers lay on my bed, hurt, there was no way of knowing whether the visitor on the window balcony had been Broad or Riley or Rogers—except that Riley had been at the door at the same moment that the man had been on the balcony.

Or had he been? I tried to remember whether I had seen the man on the balcony at the same minute that Riley's paper had come in at the door. Of course I had, but I was all mixed up. And that's how we were when Burke took charge of the meeting. And from that time on, he ran everything, including us.

Broad was sitting in the big chair. He looked not at all upset after his part of the tussle with Rogers. I wasn't sure even yet where all of the men had come from so suddenly.

Burke said: "I'm going to take, one by one, all of the possible murderers. I want it understood that at this point I am making no accusation. I am simply talking the crimes out, suggesting ways in which each of you could have committed the murders—and reasons why each of you may have done it. This is not official."

Nobody said anything. Dulcy opened her mouth for one of her celebrated screams, but Burke frowned at her, and she closed it again.

"Six persons are left here, so far untouched by the murderer. Seven with Betty, Torrence's wife. She, however, was under guard during several of the murders and has had no opportunity for those and no motive for any except the death of Miss Lizzie. But she is not guilty of Miss Lizzie's death. As a matter of fact, she suspects her own husband of the death of his aunt. But her husband is not guilty, either. Come in, Torry, and speak for yourself."

We all turned to the door to see Torry and Betty coming in. Broad gave them the big chair and perched himself insecurely on a small table. Torry was pale but seemed otherwise all right. Betty hovered over him like a mother hen protecting an oversize chick.

"I came down the fire-escape when I left Aunt Lizzie," he explained. "I was so angry at her that I didn't realize that I had come to the last step of the ladder to Jane's balcony. I stumbled. I must have hit my head against the railing. I don't remember much after that. I came to twice. Once it was storming and a man was bending over me. I couldn't see his face well, but it looked like Henry. And then he had a cup or something in his hand, and I guess you'll think it was crazy, but I got the impression that he was trying to catch the blood that came from a gash in my arm and the one on my head. Then he hit me again, with something heavy. The second time I came to, somebody was feeling in my pockets as if to rob me. But my head hurt and I couldn't protest. That's all I know."

"You're sure that it was Henry?" Burke was insistent.

"The features were like Henry's, but the face looked stiff, almost like a mask."

"That's it," said Burke with satisfaction. "That's all, Torry. You and your wife can go back up to your rooms if you want to. We have everything we need from you."

Broad took the chair again. "Mrs. Meyer," Burke said loudly, to the deaf woman, "you will tell us now about Madame Terracci. She was your sister, wasn't she, and Dulcy and Kay Johnson are your daughters, aren't they?"

A little moan came from Mrs. Meyer, but she nodded. "You are right. They never knew it. I left them with my mother back home when they were little. Kay was a good child, but Dulcy was the flighty one. She ran away to go on the stage, and then she fell in love and got herself into one mess after another, but I always hoped that she would marry a good man and settle down some day."

"Your mother sent her to stay here in this house, telling her that you were an old friend? And Kay knew that she was your daughter?" Burke was gentle but spoke loudly.

"Kay was a great comfort to me," said Mrs. Meyer, looking at Dulcy hopefully. Dulcy's face was as stiff as the mask about which they had talked. She did not look at her mother.

I tried in vain to see some resemblance between the young woman and the older one. "You saw Henry coming out of Dulcy's room one night, and then the next day you heard them quarreling because Henry wanted to marry Dulcy and Dulcy didn't want to." Burke was still gentle but firm. He had the whole business at his fingertips now. I wondered how much was fact and how much a guess.

"Yes," whispered Mrs. Meyer. Then she leaned across the space between them and put a hand on Dulcy's. "I've wanted my children for so long." But Dulcy sat still.

"Then," said Burke loudly, relentlessly, "you were certain that Dulcy had murdered Henry because he forced himself upon her, and Miss Lizzie because she, a prying gossip, had been watching her too closely and knew what had happened."

"God help me, I thought that she was the murderer," Mrs. Meyer said. "And Henry's ghost came—"

"There was no ghost. There was only this," shouted Burke, and he held up a mask. It was like a child's false face except that it was more solid. And the features were the features of Henry.

A throaty sob came from Dulcy, and then, to my amazement, she went to her mother and sank down at her feet, putting her head down in her mother's lap. Dulcy was crying. This time there was sincerity in her tears. And she

wasn't alone. Never any more would Dulcy be the predatory young female she had seemed to me. Because now she
had found that she belonged somewhere, and that somebody loved her enough to protect her even though she had
thought her guilty.

"Dulcy is not guilty of murder," Burke said. "She did
take the flavoring bottle from Jane because she thought
that it was the poison. But she left the bottle on the upstairs windowsill after she smelled it and discovered it was
harmless. Dulcy knew poisons, because Henry had told
her about them. All of these poisons came from Henry's
collection. As a drug clerk he managed, from time to time,
to abstract minute quantities of several poisons, and he
used to tantalize Dulcy by telling her what he would do
with the poisons if she didn't marry him. Isn't this true,
Dulcy?" Dulcy nodded. Her affirmative answer was muf-
fled by the black velvet of her mother's skirt.

It wasn't until later that I found out how Burke had
been hounded by the police department and the D.A.'s
office. He had grabbed at the chance to settle the cases
undercover, at night, as soon as he thought he had all the
pieces fitting together. I want to emphasize right here that
this wasn't an official investigation, that he probably had
no right at the time to make all of these people sit there
and answer his questions against their will.

The D.A. and Burke had almost come to blows about
the way this case had been handled, according to Riley,
but of course I didn't know about that then. It all seemed
perfectly natural to me. Burke was a policeman and he had
a right to ask questions, and we had to answer them.

Burke said then: "Henry was undoubtedly a little insane
on the subject of poisons. He had neat plans all worked
out on paper, and little bottles and boxes carefully labelled and put away in a small metal filing box. There was
even a list of victims with names of poisons attached. All

that the murderer had to do was to follow these directions, taking the poisons as he needed them, but of course using the names of his own chosen victims."

"Cold-blooded, and rather clever, wasn't he?" Broad put in, studying the limp figure of Rogers on the bed. "But where did Henry keep these poisons? I never saw them, and he and George were my roommates, you know."

"There was a locked drawer in a desk big enough to hold the filing box. And after Henry's death the box was kept in the cellar hole behind the coal bin, beside the glass cupboard in which George's body was found. There were no fingerprints on the box, not even Henry's. But there would be no possibility of any other poison murder with this same murderer and these same poisons, after the box was taken into custody by the police, unless the murderer kept out some poison for later use."

"There are some other things that bothered us," continued Burke thoughtfully. "What connection was there between the murder victims? Why should these persons have been chosen instead of you, the rest of you, in the house? There are two possibilities. One is the obvious one of blackmail."

I looked at Riley, who looked back at me triumphantly. "Blackmail," he repeated.

"It is entirely possible that the murderer has been blackmailing many persons in this house and that they threatened to reveal him to the police. He murdered one of them, and then the others, one by one, became so troublesome that he thought that he couldn't die more than once for a murder, so he might as well clear his path of all of these people who bothered him. This is the easiest assumption. The murderer in this case would be somebody in a position to know everything about everybody in the house—the landlady, say, or the mailman."

Mrs. Meyer looked up, startled, and Broad arose and walked over to look down carefully at the features of the mailman. "He doesn't look like a murderer," said Broad.

"Very few murderers look like murderers," said Burke. "Now this is one possible motive, this blackmail. Sit down, Broad. Rogers is still alive. The doctor has done everything he can. If he is the murderer, we can take care of him."

Broad sat down again. "There is still one more motive," continued Burke. "Suppose that our murderer killed Henry because he knew that Henry was planning to kill him. Desperately, then, he tried to get away from the house by way of the fire-escape. As he came down the iron ladder from the second floor to the first, he did not know that on the balcony there was another man, Torry, fleeing from his own anger against his Aunt Lizzie."

The room was so still that I could hear Rogers' shallow breathing from my bed. Nobody moved. Everybody watched Burke.

"It was not murder or even attempted murder this time," Burke went on. "It was an accident that the iron ladder, as it came down under the tread of the murderer, struck Torry on the head. In a panic, the murderer looked at him, thought that he was dead, and made a desperate mistake.

"The body was outside the window of Jane's room. The murderer disliked Jane. He was one of those men to whom she had paid no attention during her stay in New York."

Everybody looked at me, but I felt blank. I hadn't really paid much attention to any of the men before that stormy night. I could still hear Rogers breathing. Could he have hated me enough to want to accuse me of his own murderous crime just because I hadn't paid any attention to him?

Burke was relentless, but as casual in his tone as a nurse telling a fairy tale to a child: "The window was open and

Jane was asleep. She had heard nothing of the accident, which had been singularly noiseless. Remember that the thunder was already loud, and that any extra noises might have been considered part of that in case Jane awoke.

"Some additional way had to be found to tie this accident to Jane. The murderer saw a cup alongside of the rubber plant on the window ledge. The cup had undoubtedly been used to water the rubber plant. He used it to catch the blood that dripped from the gash in Torry's head and arm. Torry half awoke when he did this, and the murderer, half crazed, struck him on the head with something. We haven't found out yet what it is. He may even have used the heel of his shoe.

"Then it occurred to the murderer that a splash of blood somewhere in Jane's room mightn't be enough. Therefore on impulse he thrust a hand into Torry's pocket to see whether Torry had any coins that could be dipped into the blood and then tossed into Jane's room. This was a clever bit of rather twisted notion. Torry had very little change, so the murderer took all of his own change out of his pocket and thrust it into the cup that held just the little blood he had been able to get from Torry. Remember that the murderer of Henry considered that he was also the murderer of Torry."

Riley and Broad started, at almost the same minute, to ask questions, but Burke held up his hand. "Let me finish," he said. "It's a long story, but every point is carefully studied, based on evidence just as careful. The murderer stepped into the room and threw the coins to the floor. One of the dimes went into Jane's bathrobe pocket where it left a small bloodspot. Later the murderer found an opportunity to get the cup with a little more blood in it from the window ledge where he had left it, and he splashed it on Jane's mantelpiece. By this time the blood was a little diluted with the rain, which made for the fact that it was slowly coagulating. But that came later. Now, after dropping the coins and setting the cup on the window ledge beside the body, which he thought completely lifeless, he managed to close the window from the outside. Not completely, however, because he left it open so that he could get at the cup from the inside or the outside. Remember that. We'll come back to it."

All of this sounded so terribly elaborate, I thought, and I said so to Burke. He nodded. "That's the way everything was done, in the whole case. The murderer is a person who does all things in this same elaborate way. In his efforts to set the stage carefully for this and the other murders, he revealed a sense of the dramatic that comes out equally well in some of the other things he did.

"We know about Henry and Torry. Now the murderer was free to go his own way, which he did. He went back up the ladder and kept it down so that he could use it again if necessary. Remember, this is one of the fire-escapes that works with a lock catch, so that it stays down or up at the will of the people who handle it.

"At the head of the fire-escape the murderer met Miss Lizzie. She had been looking out, watching Torry go down, and she had undoubtedly seen everything that happened. This sealed Miss Lizzie's death.

"The murderer begged her to go into her room with him, to pray for him. He knew that Miss Lizzie belonged to one of these odd and unconventional sects with praying habits of its own. He told her frankly that he intended to kill himself because he was guilty of murder. But he didn't want to die without prayers and he wanted Miss Lizzie to pray with him."

Riley spoke. "That was just like her. She'd have enjoyed every minute of that."

"The murderer said that he was going to his room to get the poison that he intended using and promised that he would take it after the prayer, but that the poison would take long enough to act before death so that he could get back to his own room."

"But it was so theatrical. Surely you don't believe that it happened that way," protested Broad, looking at Rogers' quiet figure as if he wondered how a man who looked like this could have formulated such plans.

"The murderer was a dramatist, an artist. He did things elaborately, like setting a stage or designing a tapestry, or making a mask with small bits of paper soaked in wet paste and applied to a plaster model of Henry's face. The murderer was an artist."

"I still think that you're mistaken. It couldn't have happened like that," Broad said, and Riley agreed:

"It's too dramatic a story for anything except fiction or a stage or screen."

But Burke shook his head. "The artist in drama went on his murderous way," he said. "He brought two little bottles from Henry's room. But into his pocket he put the large filing box, which by the way wasn't really very large. It takes very little poison to murder many people. The box fit into the murderer's pocket, but in his hand he held one of the bottles, and in his other pocket he put the other. We have discovered traces of the poisons, in the pocket. The murderer and Miss Lizzie knelt in prayer. On her knees, with her handkerchief raised to her eyes to hide their gloating interest in what she was about to see, Miss Lizzie probably asked: 'What poison are you using?'

"'A simple poison, harmless unless taken by mouth. I'll drink it from the bottle while you pray. Smell it if you want to. It won't hurt you.' Quickly, in some way, he managed to get the chloroform under Miss Lizzie's nose, and in so doing spilled some on her handkerchief. She was alive, but unconscious, still kneeling between the bed and a chair. These kept her from falling later. I don't know exactly how the phosphorous poison was administered, but it was. And the murderer had killed, he thought, three people, with no trouble at all, and had left a clear trail. Torry he had blamed on Jane. Henry and Lizzie were enemies. Henry had written a letter in which he announced his intention of killing Miss Lizzie and then himself. That would leave the murderer free of suspicion, he thought."

"Is this all a brilliant guess," suggested Broad, "or did Rogers confess?"

"I'll answer that later," Burke replied. "Now the murderer went on his way without realizing that he had left a trail that several persons would see, later."

"And those persons were the ones he killed or tried to kill later," added Riley. "Kay Johnson, George, Madame Terracci, Broad. Broad could tell us. What did you see that you shouldn't have seen, Broad? Something you saw caused the attempt at your murder."

"I haven't an idea. It's all a blank to me," answered Broad.

Burke went on: "Leaving the room, the murderer met George. Knowing that he must have a chance to get away and create an alibi for himself, he decided that George must die under circumstances that might leave his death undiscovered for a long time and might make the police consider him a murderer if the trail already left was not enough. He told George that he had heard a prowler in the cellar. He led him downstairs, through the coal hole and into the old wine cellar where George's body was later found. It was easy enough to strike George on the head and to administer the poison before he was completely conscious again. Then, even before death, George was packed into the tight glass cupboard that was probably once a store showcase. The poison box was left at the same place and the murderer walked out, free to discard such of his clothes as had become dirty with the coal, to wash up, to be astonished when the murders were discovered.

"Later when Madame Terracci asked for an explanation of something she saw him doing with the mask the night of the first murder, he knew that he must kill her. He asked, probably, to be taught her method of pancake making, while he told the story in his own room, in order to get the poison into her. Then he took the body to her room and set the stage, to try to persuade the police that Jane was again the murderer. Unfortunately for him he didn't know that there are different ways of mixing pancake batter, even if you follow directions on the flour box, and that there is more than one way of opening a jelly glass with fingerprints already on it."

I heard a sob from Dulcy, but she said nothing. Cahoots Smith said: "There is no justice in your handling of this case. These methods would never have been permitted on the force in my day."

Burke paid no attention to him. I noticed that Rogers was stirring a little. Mrs. Meyer stroked Dulcy's bright hair. Broad settled himself more comfortably in his chair. I wondered how he felt. After all, this mysterious murderer had almost caused his death as well as that of the other victims.

"Kay Johnson took her poison in fish. She was greedy. She always took a little extra portion of food while she was cooking. The murderer came in and asked for the recipe, I think, or for something that would take her away from the table where she was eating. He added the poison to her small portion of fish, not to the main dish that Dulcy would share. He liked Dulcy and didn't want her to die. Later, after Dulcy, thinking that Jane had poisoned the bottle, took the flavoring, the murderer found it easy enough to add the residue of what had poisoned Kay and to throw the bottle where it was later found."

"A brilliant piece of fiction, Burke," Broad said lazily. "It wouldn't hold water in court, but it sounds well when you tell it."

"I have more evidence than I need. And tonight I got the last bit of evidence—here, on the balcony, tonight. I was watching. I saw everything—everything."

Riley stirred a little restlessly, and I was suddenly frightened. Could it be that Riley was the murderer instead of Rogers? But after all, maybe he was just restless because he wanted to get out and phone his paper.

Smith put in: "Absurd. This doesn't answer the questions. I thought I saw Jane going toward Madame Terracci's room. She's little and she's pretty and she can fool you or a jury. She's the murderer, and you won't see it because you don't want to. Dulcy saw her. So did I."

But Dulcy shook her yellow head. "I was just trying to make it harder for her. I lied about her because I thought she was trying to get off with all the men. And later she didn't even introduce those others that she called her brothers. I was just jealous. Jane ain't guilty."

Smith subsided into a rumble, and I realized that this was just one more case of his cahoots. He had to know more than the police or he couldn't be happy. But he wasn't the murderer, because the man who had stood outside on my balcony, trying to get at me, was tall, and Smith wasn't.

Burke went on: "A bit of the crisp brown pancake was found in the murderer's room, on the brown linoleum where it had escaped his eye. The griddle was carefully washed and put away, and so were the pancake ingredients. The murderer and Jane were the only two in the house who knew what the pancake edge was when I produced it. The murderer lied about it, giving such a farfetched idea that I knew he was lying."

Riley? Riley had called it starched lace from a brown dress.

"I haven't been able, so far," said Burke, "to trace to the murderer the telegram that was sent to Jane to accuse her of murder, but the routine works well. That would have

been almost as easy for the murderer as putting Jane's button under the box of perfectly good chocolates in Madame
Terracci's room. He knew about the will, by the way, which
is one of the reasons why he wanted Jane to be friendly."

"You will see by this time that we have covered almost all the points in question," said Burke. "The D.A.
has these, although he does not yet know about the fight
on the balcony tonight that was the climax of the plot.
You see, Rogers has been trying to get to Jane for some
time. He doubted my story of the smallpox, which was,
of course, a manufactured illness, and he has been trying
to get to Jane to warn her. Tonight he was on her balcony
for an hour, and twice Riley chased him away from there."

"He wanted to warn her against himself!" Broad put in,
more excited than I had seen him so far.

"No, Mr. Bill Broad. He wanted to warn her against
you," said Burke quietly.

Bill Broad sat up straight with an incredulous look on
his handsome face.

"But Broad was one of the victims of the murderer. You
just saved him in time," Riley insisted.

"Broad took a small amount of the poison when he
heard us ready to come into the room. He knew that he
would be saved, and thought that the poisoning would
automatically clear him of suspicion of murder in the eyes
of the law. But the eyes of the law are sharp. We have evidence enough to put you in the chair, Broad."

"You won't agree that the mailman probably did the
whole business because he was blackmailing and the victims objected?" offered Broad.

"No. The evidence points to you, Broad—every point.
You are the artist, the dramatist. You made the mask of
Henry, to frighten him. Then you killed him when he tried
to kill you. You thought that you killed Torry. You killed
Miss Lizzie. You came into Jane's room with Jane and

Riley and disappeared after you had taken the cup from the window sill and splashed the blood on the mantelpiece. The cup was found in the cellar with your coal-spotted coat, away in a corner, safely hidden. You killed Madame Terracci with poisoned pancakes and Kay Johnson with poisoned fish and with a slower acting poison than any you used except on yourself."

"You have no evidence." Broad didn't seem upset.

"No? Not your coat and hat? Not your fingerprint on George's collar? Not your fingerprint on the pancake griddle in Madame Terracci's room?" Burke sounded casual again.

"But there could have been no fingerprints," Broad said with satisfaction. Then he added, as if the words were pulled out of him: "I wore gloves."

And then everything happened at once. He made a leap toward the balcony and Curly made a leap at him. Riley and Curly grabbed him, and the policemen had him out of the room and out of the house before the doctor sent off poor Rogers to the hospital. Rogers had obviously been hit by Broad in that final big scene when the spotlight was on the mailman for possibly the first time in his life. It had been only too easy for Broad to make some of us think that he had hit Rogers to keep him from killing me from the balcony.

And he almost got away with everything. Up until the time that he took his own poison, Burke and Riley had him slated as the murderer. Then they switched around and built up a pretty case against the mailman. Motive: Blackmail.

But little by little the details came to light until Burke saw as clear a picture developing before him as he had ever caught. He held all the aces, as he said, after the coat, hat and cup were found under the coal pile near George's body.

The smallpox trick was bait, of course, but it was also protection for me, because Broad strangely blamed me for half his troubles, since I hadn't fallen for him the way all the other women did, including Dulcy. "Milton" was Bill, and I remembered hearing her cry "Milton" when she quarreled with Henry. The mask had been worn by Broad in case anybody saw him leave the house. Later he used it to frighten Mrs. Meyer.

As a reporter Riley turned out to be a fair policeman, after he went to the police school, even if he had picked the wrong murderer. And all the rest of the time I was in New York I cooked at least one meal a week for Burke and he told me all sorts of details about cases, because he said my ignorance on police matters was so strong that it gave him real inspiration.

Coachwhip Publications
CoachwhipBooks.com

The Hollow Tree Mystery

MADELON ST. DENIS

The Jekyll-Hyde Murder Case

MADELON ST. DENIS

THE DEATH KISS

MADELON ST. DENIS

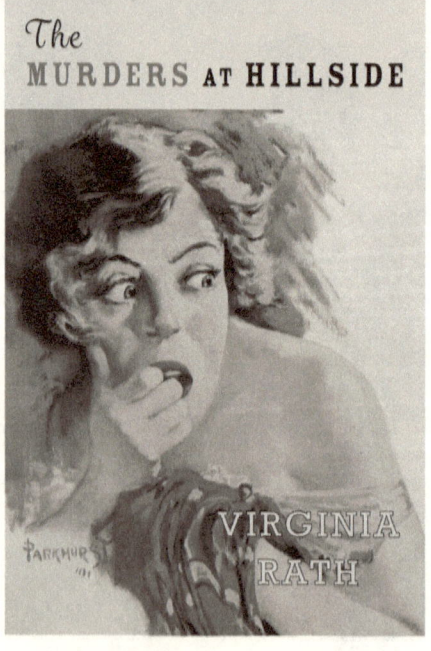

The MURDERS AT HILLSIDE

VIRGINIA RATH

Coachwhip Publications
CoachwhipBooks.com

DEATH DOWN EAST

Eleanor Blake

HELEN BURNHAM

THE MURDER OF
LALLA LEE

—

THE TELLTALE
TELEGRAM

HIDE AND GO SEEK

with, GOING TO ST. IVES

HOTEL

COLVER HARRIS

A JUDGE MASSIE
MYSTERY

THE CORPSE IS
INDIGNANT

DOUGLAS STAPLETON
and HELEN A. CAREY

Coachwhip Publications
CoachwhipBooks.com

THE FIRES AT FITCH'S FOLLY

KENNETH WHIPPLE

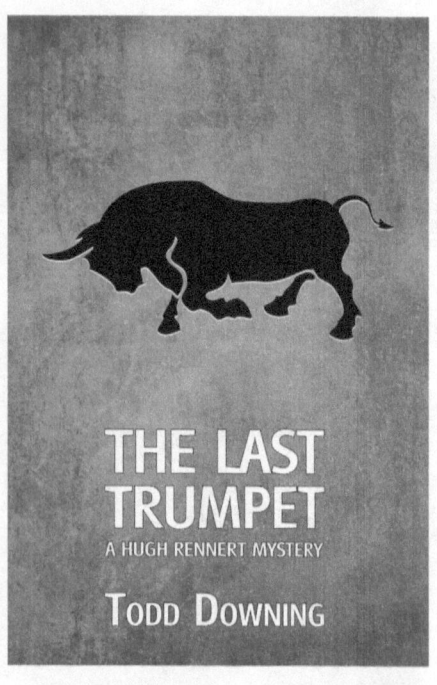

THE LAST TRUMPET

A HUGH RENNERT MYSTERY

TODD DOWNING

Jack Dolph

MURDER MAKES THE MARE GO

BLOOD-RED DEATH

MINNA BARDON

Coachwhip Publications
CoachwhipBooks.com

KILL 'EM WITH KINDNESS

By FRED DICKENSON

LADY IN LILAC

SUSANNAH SHANE

The Railroad Murder Case

R. M. LAURENSON

SULTAN'S HAREM MYSTERY

Drink the Green Water
The Milkmaid's Millions

HUGH AUSTIN

Coachwhip Publications
CoachwhipBooks.com

LOUIS F. BOOTH

THE BANK VAULT MYSTERY
BROKERS' END

MURDER IN THE
FAMILY

NICE
PEOPLE
MURDER

Mary Hastings Bradley

BLOOD ON HER SHOE

MEDORA FIELD

MURDER AT
DRAKE'S ANCHORAGE

E. LEE WADDELL

Coachwhip Publications
CoachwhipBooks.com

3 DETECTIVES
MURDER
ON THE RAILS
WHITECHURCH • THORNE
• TORGERSON

MURDER
A LA
MODE

ELEANORE
KELLY
SELLARS

CLASSIC RED BADGE PRIZE MYSTERY

MURDER
IN TEXAS

Ada E. Lingo

"The story of a big-time murder in
a small town, with the atmosphere
of a hard-boiled newspaper office,
a background of 'hot oil' and
sudden gushers, and the intensity
of a Texas heat wave."

MURDER
IN A WALLED TOWN
KATHERINE WOODS

Coachwhip Publications
CoachwhipBooks.com

www.ingramcontent.com/pod-product-compliance
Lightning Source LLC
Chambersburg PA
CBHW020837260626
47169CB00003B/1027